Astral Bodies

JAY MERILL was born in Warwickshire and now lives in London. She attended the University of London and works as a freelance editor. Her short stories have been published in a wide number of literary magazines in the UK and USA.

Astral Bodies

JAY MERILL

SALT

CAMBRIDGE

PUBLISHED BY SALT PUBLISHING
PO Box 937, Great Wilbraham. Cambridge PDO CB21 5JX United Kingdom

First published 2007

Printed and bound in the United Kingdom by Lightning Source

Typeset in Swift 9.5/13

ISBN 978 1 84471 318 9 paperback

Salt Publishing Ltd gratefully acknowledges
the financial assistance of Arts Council England

1 3 5 7 9 8 6 4 2

For Avrina

Contents

Beacon   1

Yellow Plastic Shoe   8

The Other Side of Diane   12

Blue Movie   18

The Outsider   21

Salamander   30

Tango   44

Chicken eye   48

Billie Ricky   58

WatchTower   63

The Girl Can't Help It   73

TailBacks   81

The Sadness Story   87

Astral Bodies   92

Lady of the Spin   100

Waving with Rabbit   103

Monkey Face   111

The Gold-Road   115

Acknowledgements   119

Beacon

The plant on my windowsill has died, shame that, Tilly gave it to me the last time she was over. I feel bad about it but what can I do, I've never had green fingers. Tilly said it would get gold coloured flowers when summer came but it'll never flower now. I can hear skateboarders from outside the window, that rattling glide and the crash as they land after a jump, or else it's the shutters going up on the line of garages, grate of corrugated metal and the bang as they reach the top. Sometimes it's hard to tell what sounds are.

Mr Smith had paws on him soft and yellow as plums. Tilly told me, pulling a face which said he was a sickly poisonous fruit. We were living in Leicester, same as now and Tilly used to go round to the Smiths' babysitting after school. She was going to be an actress and needed to save up for this drama course. It's history the way he used to poke at her when the wife was frying chips for tea. Behind the sofa they'd go, she in her school knickers, Mr Smith being turned on by that, her knickers getting wet in the crotch before he even touched her, but it wasn't that she liked him. He was too smooth by half and there was this moist-sticky something about his whole personality. Quite unpalatable really, we used to shiver and laugh about it, though she liked

[1]

the way she felt about herself when she was with him. She was turned on by this sense of power, but there was also something terrifying. She shook her head and tried to pinpoint what it was. Well, it had something to do with seeing there were more things going on all the time than what you saw at first, levels behind levels. You didn't know the truth of things. As if the world you could see was just a fake and the real one was hidden from view. A scary idea but one which got her thinking, there was some appeal to it. Being an adult was seeing that things weren't at all as they seemed, they could be quite the opposite.

Then there'd been Daniel, a boy from her school. Daniel was also not what he seemed but in a different way. Instead of the soft paddy pawing there'd been grasping claws. He'd turned from sweet to rough more quickly than you can imagine. She'd met up with him at the recreation ground when she was bunking off from school. He'd been all smiley-warm. Just the dinner hour, nothing too drastic, she'd stood in front of him, chips between them. It's funny Tilly says now, how chips seemed to be a part of every sorrow. By then she was well on the way to becoming an actress, in her mind at least, and it's far from clear whether she was the same Tilly as she was behind the couch in the house of the Smiths on babysitting afternoons. She'd felt more and she'd felt less, all at the same time. Daniel was a brawn-brain, Tilly said later. He was affecting casualness for the sake of easy victory, but he was the idol of many girls at school and this gave him sex appeal. Daniel was sweet and smiling, if anything over-polite. She brought him into her house one lunchtime when she knew her Aunt Al was out and not likely to be back for hours and this was asking for trouble. Autumn, new term, a time of blackberries on the edge of the recreation ground. He'd hung by her back gate longingly and she'd agreed he could come in. In the cool empty dining room off the kitchen, he'd dragged her to the floor and raped her pure and simple, fucking her hard by the feet of the table, clamping her jaw down tight with his hand as if she wasn't human, but just this piece of junk he'd come across. She could smell him salty with rage and hatred, a different Daniel from the one he put out to the world. When he'd come he let her go and she crawled towards the hallway, hoping to make it to the bathroom, a smear of blood connecting her to carpet, to wood.

Aunt Al later, having one of her fits about the way the world treated her, today it was that the bus hadn't stopped for her, it had splashed her instead. She had mud splattered up the side of her coat, not that the coat was in any way new, if she had it cleaned, in fact, it would fall to pieces. So she was in no mood to notice a bit of blood and the misplacement of doormats, she'd sobbed in her room and then come down to sit at the end of the table and scratch her psoriasis. Discs of dry red flesh appeared all over her arms as skin flakes fell to the floor. The same floor where earlier Tilly had been raped. She looked round the room and it seemed a different place with the light on and the TV on and the curtains drawn together. And yet the rape *had* happened here. Tilly straightened the dishevelled doormat and went to have a bath. At school the next day Daniel was easy and polite as usual, being chatted up by a group of girls. He waved at Tilly as she passed him in the corridor.

If you swapped around the a and the e in 'Daniel' you'd have the word 'denial' in front of your eyes. It pleased her that his name contained the letters of his perfidy. She looked right past him.

Tilly says herself she looked far more of a kid than she was then and this was due to Aunt Al who hadn't caught on that Tilly was growing up and was something called a *teenager*. Tilly wore her school clothes all the time, her breasts pushing against the unaccommodating straightness of her shirts. In her winter coat she looked like a frump, the hairy material between the buttons stretched back till there was a gap, the arms finishing short, above her wrists. Aunt Al was self-absorbed and wouldn't have seen any of this, besides which it wasn't in her interest to admit she had a teenager on her hands. Then one night I got this phone call and Tilly said she wasn't at her aunt's, she wasn't even in Leicester at all. Where was she? Coventry. What was Tilly doing there? She was at her Dad's.

In a couple of weeks Tilly came back again, but she was a different girl. She was cool and glam and had her hair cut in this floppy-wispy way that everybody envied. Aunt Al hid in her room for a day or two then got over it and went back to being Mrs Oblivious of everything outside her own concerns. Tilly hadn't heard from her Dad since the age of five and then out of the blue he'd sent a letter to Aunt Al saying he was married with a wife and child. Yes, there was even a younger sister. He and the wife Pauline had come and picked Tilly up by car one day and the thing that made her laugh about it was that Mr Smith had seen her getting in the car down the street and thought she'd been abducted. His smooth fruity face looked furrowed and orange with fright. What did he think? That Tilly'd gone off with some strange couple, that the man would use her for sexual purposes when the wife was in the kitchen? We laughed over this one till we cried.

Tilly kept making this sighing noise after she got back from Coventry. It was because of all the stuff she'd been surrounded with. Quilted stuff and leathery stuff and heavy wood and thick spongy carpets. Into which you sank. And she'd had her own ensuite bathroom, mahogany and chrome, and a bed with six pillows. She'd found it a bit creepy that room and she'd had to keep checking under the bed to make sure there was nothing hiding there. She always looked behind the dressing table last thing at night. Tilly collapsed her jaw inwards as she got on to the subject of the furniture.

'Furniture,' I said. 'Well there has to be furniture.'

'But there was so *much* of it,' Tilly said with a look.

She said she'd felt oppressed and being there had made her see the beauty of empty space. She went on about how she was tempted to throw out her own wardrobe and her bedside chair. She pulled a face as if to say you never knew what horrors they might be concealing. She never used to think about these objects but now the sight of them made her feel uneasy.

If there were too many things everywhere, Tilly said, you'd be unable to see what was going on around you, most probably you'd hardly even see yourself. She was grateful for having gone to Coventry, it had opened her eyes to what could happen to you if you weren't on your guard. Because let's face it, it was a world so easy and comfortable to slip into. Tilly had a look of terror on her face when she said this, as though she was picturing its softness as something which might dissolve you. Being in Coventry, Tilly said, gave her the feeling of being buried alive, as if she were pinned down underneath a mountain and couldn't see what was really happening in the world.

'Furniture.' Tilly said, was an unbearable thought. She said it was something which gave you a false sense of security. You couldn't trust it, it was only a façade. There was no real substance despite what some people might think. She said she had to get away from all of that. Pauline, Tilly told me, was always cleaning furniture and worrying in case it ended up scratched. It was, *Don't put your feet on the seats, don't put that cup down on the table!* the whole time Tilly was in Coventry. Imagine living like that permanently.

Tilly loved going over how there were three TVs in her Dad's house, and gadgets for every kind of thing you'd never have thought of getting into if nobody'd invented them. Curling your hair and straightening your hair and making waffles.

For Tilly, by far the most awful thing was that her little sister, Moira, had all of this furniture in miniature for her Barbies. There Moira'd sit, surrounded by all the stuff of her miniature universe. Tilly felt as if she was being smothered, all she could think of was breaking free. This wasn't an easy thought at first though, because the smothered feeling was quite seductive and with every day that passed she felt there was less breath left in her to resist. If she hadn't just been on holiday she'd have been in real danger. That's why she was sighing now, Tilly realised. Those long wisps of hair curving towards her cheeks fluttered outwards each time this happened. The sighing was thankful rather than hopeless, she was sighing with relief that she could still breathe.

Just after Coventry Tilly met up with Shuri and Lee, a homeless couple. She hung on to the belief that sleeping rough was some kind of choice they'd made and looked on them as heroic types for quite some time. As if they wanted to be out in some doorway all weathers in thin sleeping bags over cardboard moist with piss, breathing in the stench of rotten air. But Tilly didn't want to give up the idea of the noble purity of what they were doing and kept on ignoring the fact that Shuri and Lee had problems that always seemed to stop them getting anything together. They were artists, Tilly used to say defiantly. And she'd sit for hours with them in the pub talking about painting pictures and selling them to make enough dosh to live on and buying a van maybe, that they could kit out and store their paints in. Well, a van wasn't a house, was it, said Tilly, looking a bit uneasy even so at the way she was planning for the perfect pair to start getting into the ownership game. Her voice flagged then she said with more spirit how they wouldn't have to have any furniture inside, and could paint it a good colour, make it bright and artistic, and habitable. It'd be better than the street and they'd be expressing themselves. We were all in the pub, all getting beyond it by this time, but even so I had the distinct feeling Shuri and Lee were willing to go along with anything for the sake of the rounds of booze Tilly was getting in. We were in the pub most nights. Tilly was full of ideas for the pair of them. One day she came round to mine with a white face and said she'd been deceiving herself, she'd been wrong. It was a wrench seeing that, but she said she couldn't go on thinking such a cock-eyed thought as that they'd chosen to live in a doorway. It turned out Shuri had stabbed Lee in the leg in a fight over some drugs she said he'd stolen and Lee'd had a go at Tilly, demanding money, in spite of the fact she didn't have a bean. Tilly was quite down about it for some time but then she started getting her bright look back and admitted she'd been so busy looking beyond the surface that she couldn't see what was in front of her nose. And it all went to prove that the truth could turn out to be what was obvious as easily as what was not. How was that for irony? Tilly said it did her head in. She said she realised now that the truth could be anywhere, if only you could see.

Harsh metallic clanking outside my window. A car driving over the gratings in the road, bins being trundled out to the street? Is it a Monday, when the rubbish is collected, I haven't put mine out. But no, it's Saturday, surely. I look up at the glass, too lazy to get out of bed. Sad the plant's had it, it's gone all brown and limp, looks beyond saving. Was it too much water or not enough that did this? I was looking forward to seeing the flowers – from what Tilly said, they were something special. The noise of scraping metal is getting louder, it's making my head hurt, I'll never get back to sleep if it carries on. I think of getting up to put on the coffee, yawning into my sleeve. Another late night. Then I notice the rattling is right outside now and I pull myself up and drag back the curtains. I see a supermarket trolley standing on the little concrete frontage and Tilly, of all people, guiding its wonky wheels round towards my door. Haven't seen her for weeks, not since she brought the plant round. I let her in and get back into bed, it's so cold out. She manoeuvres the trolley into the hall and comes and sits at my feet. Turns out she's about to go on holiday and her car's broken down and she had a load of stuff she wanted to bring over. I don't ask her if she'd ever heard of a taxi, because Tilly's the sort who always has to go about things in her own way. She tells me she's given up the idea of acting, she's thought about it and decided it isn't right for her, it's not the direction she wants to be taking.

She gives a sudden scream of anguish and I know she's noticed the plant, which though I haven't said so was luscious and gorgeous and flourishing when she'd brought it.

'And look at it now!' Tilly cries out.

I tell her I do feel sad about it and I really am upset I'll never get to see the flowers and she's quiet for a bit and looks as if she's thinking. The day's so dim and overcast by now Tilly says it needs a bit of brightening and she disappears out, coming back with a packet of pink stripy birthday candles. In the meantime I've made coffee and set it out for us with toast. Tilly ties a candle to each of the dead looking sad branches and then lights them one by one. At first they flicker and sputter, then suddenly the whole plant's shining out gold with flame. Tilly says we need a beacon to tell us where we are. From outside my window comes the call of birds or the hoot of car horns, it's not always easy to know exactly what you're hearing. I peer out of the curtain but the day's too dark to really see.

Yellow Plastic Shoe

The beachcomber drifts along by the sea looking out for things—treasures maybe, oddments, bits of this or that. She sighs dreamily enjoying salt wind in her face, and underfoot that quick shift of the sand. She's here at the water's edge, looking for that small shining something.

The sea is purple and blue, nearly all mist. What's that she sees? A tiny point of a shape which gleams just a little way ahead. What is it? The beachcomber moving across ginger stones and a flat beige lake of sand, suddenly stops. Maybe she likes the little mystery, wants to delay the moment of discovery. It's precious, that time which leads up to the finding.

In this pause she stares back at the low railings of the promenade gardens where at the same moment a dim figure is passing steadily along. The gardener. On and on, what a trudge, down the track of bare earth. Poor drab figure, the beachcomber thinks to herself with a burst of sudden ungenerous feeling. She stands still and watches. Trudging and stopping, trudging and stopping, what a fate. How hateful to be so regular, so precise. And thinking this, the beachcomber gives herself a quick inner smile, grateful to be herself. Then she turns away, brings her eyes back to the sea and the mist and the yellow gleam of the unknown object. How delicious it is this time of knowing that there is something but not what it will turn out to be.

Her heart swells at the sight of the wild shoreline and broad pale sky, while the wind whooshes her hair into flying salty strips. She looks the picture of ethereal beauty as she steps, quickly now, across the flat ginger stones whose surfaces are all glimmer and fade. And *what* if the gardener thinks of her as unrealistic. She says to herself it's only because the gardener is too limited to appreciate certain things and her consciousness has formed itself into a pattern the same shape as the flowerbeds. Her trouble is she's been trudging along that same straight furrow for years now. Earlier, crossing the promenade, the beachcomber had seen intense dislike in the gardener's eyes. Well, why worry. Still, she doesn't enjoy the idea of being condemned like that by someone, it gives her a bad feeling. She lets out a sigh, tries to put the gardener out of her mind.

And it is true, the gardener disapproves of the beachcomber, saying to herself, There's that mad woman, whenever she catches sight of her. She feels bad tempered just seeing that distant figure on the beach, drifting haphazardly, gliding along. All empty pretension, she thinks, her anger rising up. And realising that the beachcomber despises her doesn't help the gardener to be kinder in her thoughts. She's thoroughly aware that the beachcomber would despise all gardeners on principle. How impossible it would be to live without order and planning of any kind, and yet this is essentially what the beachcomber values. She just likes to drift with the tide, believes only in a munificent present, the gardener thinks as she looks down now at the beachcomber hurrying to the line of the sea. The gardener gives her head a rough shake. How totally impossible, to be always looking for unplanned beauty which will be provided by nature without any effort having been put into the process.

What really torments the gardener is the enormity of the delusion. *She's completely unaware!* she shouts out loud to the wind, and as she goes on with her planting she thinks, If I were a beachcomber I'd find more treasure than she does, because you have to be systematic, you can't go rambling all over the bloody place. She gives herself a quick smile as she moves on along her furrow, feels this sudden dart of pleasure at being up here on the promenade planting seedlings, happy in her work, loving her chosen occupation. Giving something back to nature, not just doing the taking, there's a pride in her for that. Looking up for a moment her mouth makes a definite grimace as she sees the distant beachcomber make a little fluttering lunge towards some obscure object on the sand.

The gardener stops, as she does every few paces, takes out three tiny seedlings from the bag on her shoulder and plants the first one in the pre-dug furrow. She pours out a bit of water from the plastic bottle hanging at her waist, makes sure the earth is firm and stable around the root. Then she gives three little pats of encouragement to the earth and the growing process. What does that irresponsible beachcomber know about love and caring? she thinks.

She's planted the third seedling, patted the earth to a hard compact plateau, has walked over to her barrow, replenished the stock in her shoulder bag from the seed trays, refilled her water bottle, and now she glances with satisfaction at the long line of fragile pale green plantlets all flapping in the wind. *Tender listening ears*, is how she thinks of them.

The beachcomber passes a row of terns, one swallowing a grey triangular fish, another pecking at a wormy patch of sand, a third squealing into the wind. Standing like sentinels, she thinks as she goes. She comes at last to her little bit of gold, it's a yellow plastic shoe, a child's shoe. She lifts it up, feels a fast rush of joy. Little lost shoe, so pointless, so beautiful. She swings it by the strap, swings it this way and that, at last clasping it tight against her. Finally she stands tall and poised and holds the child's shoe high into the air.

The dying sun has turned the sky bronze. The gardener straightens up, puts her hand above her eyes for focus, drops her trowel and walks to the iron railings. She climbs them and sits on the top, perching there, staring out at the wide metallic sky. She's thinking, 'here is the earth spinning through space and here I am upon the earth planting a bed of geraniums. She has this sense of being connected, feels rooted to the source of things, deeply embedded and belonging, a good feeling to have. Just then she notices the beachcomber standing with her arm outstretched. Next minute something is flung up into the air and it goes smooth and steady into an arc so wide it seems to hold all the shining bronze of the sky. It's an intuitive moment. In a movement which is almost involuntary and definitely without thought, the gardener raises her own hand and it is as though she is linked by this gesture to the tiny flying thing.

Down on the darkening sand the beachcomber looks up to see the gardener, her arm held high, and the two women exchange smiles that neither of them can see. At this second they feel as if they're both part of some single intention. Planting and finding, planting and finding. The gardener waves her hand in salute. Up above, three birds fly high on the wind, below, the sea is a torrent of choppy waves.

The Other Side of Diane

The white wellies were on a cluttered table-top. Cream-white and tiny with little puckered seaside shapes on. Such as starfish and a bucket, and seaweed and a spade. Mum wanted them for my baby sister Glenda, they were the cutest wellies I'd ever seen. When Glenda could walk she'd walk in those wellies. She'd jump and skip in those wellies, I could just picture it. Nobody else bid for them, everybody around was a friend of my mum and they were all smiling in the direction of Glenda in the buggy. Glenda herself having no idea, was just on the point of throwing out a furry bear for Diane to pick up again.

'Oh Diane, would you just get those for me?' Mum gave Diane the money for the wellies and off Diane ran to the table, to the wellie-seller.

Diane had that something bad about her that made me like her. Or not bad really, a sense of fun. She was someone I could giggle with, the giggles cascading. Maybe they would not stop, there was that feeling when we got together and the laughing started. We'd go skidding together down hallways, making the mats slip.

'Be careful you two,' Mum used to shout.

Diane was fizzy, unlike her sister Mel who was sensible. Mel was pretty, my mother said, Diane attractive. I liked *attractive* better, pretty was boring, a touch too sweet and clean. I never knew how to laugh with Mel. She smiled a lot, when chatting politely with my mum or the teachers, but that was it. Diane, if she spoke to my mother at all, or any adult, usually had a laugh behind her hand. She did a quick flicking thing with her tongue and then bunched up her lips in a smirk. Diane was somebody who could smirk and go normal the next second if an adult looked at her. Sometimes she did a routine of it on purpose, so they *would* see, bunching her lips up and then making them go straight again many times. Flick flack, flick flack.

'Don't play the fool Diane,' the teachers said. And Mel, and their mum who never smiled or laughed at all but always looked as if she was about to burst. Everybody said in fact, but me. I wondered if Diane took after her dad. He had died in an accident not very long ago, just before Diane's mum moved here. It was very sad and I expect that's why Diane's mum always looked unhappy. Nobody ever spoke about Diane's family except in a hushed voice, because of the accident.

At home Diane had an eighteen month old baby brother and when he was around she went all cooey-gooey. I couldn't understand how the brother put up with it but supposed he had no choice. Diane's baby brother's name was Robbie, and she sounded soppy and soupy saying, *Robbie, Robbie, there you are,* as if she'd expected him to be somewhere else.

But when Diane played the fool she did it better than anybody. She was especially good at mimicking teachers. Mel and I were in the third year, Diane was a year older. She walked like Mr Scope who waddled like a pig. Diane made piggy grunting noises to go with the walk. She made the face of Miss Tyne, the school secretary, and put a growl to go with it, because this was the right noise to go with her face. Miss Tyne spoke in a cold and hard voice, but behind that was a growl. Diane was the one who made us hear the growl inside her words. Miss Tyne's chin was prickly and Diane said it was because she had to shave like a man. When we heard the voice of Miss Tyne in the corridor at school it made me and Diane laugh so much we could hardly stop.

'What's the matter girls?' She'd say to us crossly. 'What are you doing in this corridor? Go to your classroom—don't run.'

'Yes Miss Tyne,' we'd go, voices quaking, hands hiding wide-mouthed laughter. Our giggles burst like bubbles through our fingers.

'Don't run,' I said.'

'No Miss Tyne.'

In the book of Greek vases at home, we scribbled wee coming out of the willies of the dark-naked figures. Dotted lines of wee which arced up and up till they reached the top of the page. It was Diane's idea. We laughed till we cried and hid the page away from my mother. That was Diane for you. Diane put the fun in dreary, she made everything fizzier than it was.

But she had her other side.

Mum in a mac because it might rain at any minute, there was that uncertainty about the day. We were going to a spring fete where you could buy things and win things. Me and Diane with Mum and my baby sister Glenda. Diane's mum wasn't with us, as when she wasn't working she seldom left the house.

'What sort of things?' I wanted to know.

'Toys, I expect.' Mum was distracted, she was carrying a bag of stuff to give to a friend who had a stall, and pushing the buggy. Diane asked if *she* could push the buggy. Her *other side* was already starting to show.

It didn't rain, the wind got quite strong and blew at us as we went along. Mum said the wind had chased the rain away. And the fete was on a hill. The awnings of the stalls blew up into the air like sails and the stallholders had to hold onto the other ends like in a tug-of-war. Glenda was eating a peach which squirted juice, then she went red and cried. Mum said she needed changing. There was a funny smell, which made me giggle. Diane did not join in. Mushy peach slobber came out of Glenda's mouth. She was teething I expect, that's what Mum usually said. I tried to amuse her with a bit of string as if she were a cat, but I soon lost interest. Babies were not so interesting as cats. But the-other-side of Diane would have disagreed.

Diane could suddenly turn motherish, with eyes of responsibility. Eyes lost to childhood, eyes full of care. I was eight, Diane nine, but just like that she became a mother-figure even so. This was a Diane I didn't understand, even the goody sensible Mel wasn't as dull as this. There she'd stand next to the buggy with a tissue at the ready, clucking at Glenda. She clucked, Glenda screamed, but it didn't put Diane off. She patted at the cover that was wrapped around Glenda's kicking legs, standing on call and ready to be of service. She passed nappies and wipes to my mum and took the dirties off to the bin. All fun forgotten, a serious-business look on her face turning her into someone I didn't want to play with. Not that she wanted to play, did she. She still hung about at the buggy when the changing was over, ready with tissues, asking my mum if she could hold the baby-drinking-cup. By now, even mum looked as if she wanted to tell Diane to run along and play.

So there was the laughing Diane and the Diane on motherhood duty, waiting at the side of buggies for toys to be dropped so she could pick them up again. Her hands itching it seemed to be picking up thrown toys, her fun side on hold, invisible. You could look at her as hard as you liked, you wouldn't discover it. All you'd see was a *how can I please you* kind of expression flickering round her lips. I thought of it as Diane's *duty-face.* In a way, Diane, with her two different parts frightened me.

Things were sold cheap in the fete. Bargains. And there was an auction. All the mothers laughed as if this was a casual thing and they didn't care if they got the things they waved for. Mum waved that she wanted this little pair of white wellies, but she was so casual and smiling, I couldn't tell if she really wanted them.

'They'll do, why not?' she said.

Other mothers stood either side of her. She waved her hand, light catching at the side of it and running down her flower-print silky arm.

Well, anyway, when Diane got the wellies for my mother she started to run back across the grass from the stall and then she stopped. She stopped moving and wouldn't start, just clung to a bit of grass with her feet and held the wellies close to her, and this look came into her face as if Robbie was somewhere near. I even looked round for him, but no sign. It was the wellies making Diane look this way. And she just stood where she was, half way across the grass, her feet firm against the ground, the white wellies pressed against her chest as if she wasn't ever going to let them go. Mum called over to her and so did quite a few of the other mothers but no use. Diane clung onto the wellies, looking zonked, at first smiling then looking frightened. But even at the frightened time clinging on tight to the wellies.

'Aren't you going to bring them?' Mum called to her, mystified.

It had all gone quiet everywhere. Diane silent and frozen looking stood alone half way across the field, her thin legs quaking. Everybody was staring at her.

She started shaking her head.

'No,' she shouted out in a cracked and trembly voice, but still defiant. Still refusing to budge.

Nobody knew what was happening.

'Why not?' Mum called into the baffled silence.

'Diane?' My mother's reasonable voice rang out, perplexed.

Then all the mothers began shouting to Diane to give up the wellies.

'Give them to her Diane. Diane!'

'The little white wellies.'

Harsh voices and soft voices, some near some further off, like a chorus rising up into the wind.

But then suddenly my mother and all her friends at the fete went quiet and I sensed they were thinking about Diane's father's accident and the way her mother had to struggle to keep the home going. They all kind of looked away from Diane. There was a bit of whispering and a few serious faces and then it was all back to normal. Talking started up and all the adults looked as if nothing funny had ever happened. Diane was forgiven and forgotten about. I can't remember if Diane walked home with us after the fete and came to tea at our house as she usually did, but I think she probably went off on her own. Some time later though, on a sunny day without any rain in sight, Robbie came round to our house with Mel and Diane. He was wearing the white wellies. Mum never said a word as Robbie hopped and pointed at his toes to show off a boat, a sea-horse, a little fish. She only laughed and gave Robbie and Glenda a slice of apple. I was glad Robbie had the wellies, because he'd lost a father and to me it seemed only fair.

Diane started off giggly but she soon turned serious, sponging up a bit of spit-out apple skin from Robbie's chin. She dabbed away with a corner of damp cloth, clucking her tongue and muttering under her breath. I looked at her to see if there was a bit of laughter lurking somewhere and tried to make contact with my eyes, but I should have known better, there was no getting through to her. Diane's *other side* had taken over completely and she was wearing her serious duty-face as if it was the only face she had. Funny how Diane could change from one thing to the other just like that. Flick flack, flick flack, flick flack.

Blue Movie

Puff drops by early out of breath, taking me a few years' back to when we were in the Home, don't want to think of that place, get a shaky feeling, start to squeak, it's just this nervous reaction I can't help having. Walking up the hill to school, Puff can't talk, it's her asthma attack, she's falling back against this wall as if she's gonna croak it, Oh shit and she's gone and forgotten her inhaler, head like a sieve, that girl. So I run back, squeaking till my throat aches, ring on the doorbell, bolt up to her room and get the thing, race right to her with this horrible but saving contraption in my hand, silver and grey; the girl's turning yellow when I get there, there's no breath left in er, I remember it. *Puff on this*, I squeak.

Puff says, *Got this idea girl, easy and everything, we could make a packet. Great thing about it is we don't have to do a fucking thing. No shit job that'll drive you crazy, make you feel like a helpless slave, you just have to stand about on a set somewhere. You show em yer fanny, wiggle yer bum and that, maybe you have to let this pervy put his finger in, so what. You wait and they say 'Take' and then it's over, there's this board with black and white stripes and that, or sometimes they'll want to replay the scene, no problem, you just stand there. Same as last time, it's so easy, you just stand there awhile and wiggle your bum and let the pervy carry on with the fingering, or maybe they'll pour this vanilla custard or something on the pervy's prick and they'll tell you to start eating it off him. Stuff like that. A Blue Movie.*

Puff says, *And that's it, that's all girl, an you get loadsa money, you'll be laughing. There'll be dosh spillin out your ears, you won't need to get one of them slave type jobs, won't have to throw yourself away or carry on with all that squeakin. It'll be heaven girl, that's what I'm tellin you. Can you hear me Squeak girl, it'll be the bee's. And can you just see us then, can you just see the pair of us. I'm tellin you, it'll be something, it really will. We can go where we like, do what we want and when we want to. You won't believe how good it'll feel till you see. An all you have to do Squeak is stand there, feel this bit of a trickle of spunk from this pervy guy, it'll be running down your leg say, but what's that anyway, you take no notice of all of that stuff, listen to me. All you have to do is just stand there and that and you'll be in the movie. Nothin to it girl, I'm tellin you how it will be.*

Puff drops by late in her purple wig, *What you do is hide upstairs an wait, easy as that girl.*

We go over it, seems okay.

I'll be coming in through the door with him, soon after eight as I can make it. Squeak, you be waiting quiet. Got that? Puff says, *It'll be a doddle, girl.*

And I say, *But what about later, when he finds his wallet's gone?*

Crap, goes Puff. *Guy won't do fuck all, he'll keep right away from Police, Won't make no trouble.*

I wonder why he won't but Puff knows about guys and stuff like this, I trust her.

Though you've got to get the timing right. I don't want to end up having to let him do it. Okay, We'll go over it again, I come in with the guy, you wait eight minutes, no ten. Then come in, yeah? We'll be in bed, trousers on the soddin chair.

Right. I get the picture but I have me doubts.

You get the dosh, girl, then you say me ol man's comin. You start screamin an that, loud as anything. Screamin not squeakin, you hear me?

Right, I say.

Puff says, *It's simple, what we do is go down this dark alley, there's two of us, he'll be pissed the guy, stupid, he'll be easy. We'll choose the* right one, drunk and fat, alone, goes without saying. We'll go in pub, pick him out, roll im when he's half way down the alley. Piece of piss.

S'posing somebody comes the minute we're rolling him?

Nah, we'll make sure. It's that simple, Squeak girl, I'm telling yer, guy'll hardly know what's happening. Be lying down by that wall docile as a dead rabbit. Done it loads of times, haven't I.

Have you, Puff?

Course I ave, right.

Right.

Puff says, Go in the changing room, pretend you're trying something. What you do is keep asking for a different size, keep em busy looking, Squeak.

Get some er them boots they got there Puff, I tell her. Think you could get some've them silver boots?

Don't make me laugh, it leaves me breathless, I'll clean the place out, nothin to it girl. You jus keep on tryin stuff an asking the woman to look and it'll be cool. Meetcha later back at mine, we'll go fifty-fifty, be rich Squeak. I'll get a load've gear, maybe do the till, keep em distracted girl, that's all. Nothin to it, believe what I'm tellin yer. You keep on tryin stuff, that's not hard, that's easy.

Right.

We're in the shop like, then there's this one hell've a row and Puff goes burstin through the door with this guy an dog after her out've nowhere, leapin out've bleedin nowhere. Bastards're lovin it, shop woman's screaming, Police, she's goin. I walk out the shop all calm, no sign've me mate.

Puff drops by later, says shoplifting aint no fucking joke, she's re-thinking her old idea about starring in a Blue Movie if I'd be up for that; says they got her belting across these friggin gardens, she'd have jumped the fence but she'd started getting wheezy, hardly any breath left inside her, an they caught her by the wig an it came off. Had to walk back along road with Police her own hair pinned flat as a squashed beetle, purple wig taken into custody. Felt such a fool girl, lookin like a bloody insect. Seen meself in shop window. Sorry sight.

The Outsider

Josie Colthanger is boozy, she's bursting with sun-heat as she comes walking down the street—if you can *call* it walking, the pattern of her route is wonky if not zigzag. Main thing is she's dizzy, that's why she skids half totters as she goes. Booze and heat together, that's what's doing it. Bright white street in empty afternoon making her feel cut off from things and, savage. She'd scream right out if it weren't for having to keep her teeth clamped tight together to stop the hiccups. Because, what a day, what a head spinning sod of a day she's stuck with.

Dad's a slab of a man who's stripy suit jacket arms are a good two inches short of his wrists, they hang like awkward cardboard cut-outs attached to shoulders by drawing pins. He's wearing this tie of iridescent cerulean blue which dangles in the gully between his lapels.

Mum herself is a bulky monument, especially about chin and neck, who sees herself as sweetly delicate in spite of the evidence. She wears a blouse with a frill of fresh salmon pink which lurches in time to her plodding footsteps.

Dad is knock kneed, splay handed, soft whirring as a moth in his movements, but there's a witch-finder's driving force at the core of him despite his tremulous little *Oh no's* of self deprecation and nodding affability. A clue hunter to the point of brutality, heart of instinctive intolerance.

Mum, inclined to be hairy, is for decency's sake, an avid wielder of the ladies' razor, in the house she's obsessed with cleanliness, constantly hoovering and applying bleaches. She's got a strong affection for the word *hygiene* and when she's feeling happy, when everything's all tidy in her kitchen, say, she'll sometimes just stand there and whisper it to herself over and over. *Hygiene.* It's got that soothing, mystery touch. Could be she's seeking validation of personal worth with these excesses, who knows. Another thing she has in abundance is an out of the way strong loathing for anybody less meticulous than *she* is in the matters of hair and dust removal.

So Josie. Here she comes tripping and slipping along on this dazzling day she just can't take. Sometimes she'll stop and mutter through tight teeth, give her lips a harsh lick, as if tasting her anger, assessing the flavour of it. She'll stand still a moment with a far off look as if she's imagining being somewhere else, then away she'll go, the yellow part of her hair, which starts three inches from the roots, flying in greasy strands all gold in the sun, a mockery of exuberance. Josie's down, feeling bleak and cut off from everything, a remote and unwanted speck in this alien street. The sun does nothing to comfort her. If anything she hates it for making her feel drab. She wants it to go away so *she* can be the bright one, or at least be left unpressured about the way she is. The sun seems to expect her to be happy. She can't live up to it.

Mum and Dad have lots in common, for a start there's a shared habitual gloating at the thought of their joint bank balance, and they both get huge life satisfaction from seeing how much more they were able to extract from a situation than had been expected. They're always having these meaningful conversations which start off with, 'Guess What!' when they've squeezed a bit more out of somebody than they'd have thought possible in the abstract. Today, sitting in the garden of an imposing Edwardian wine bar there's this pleasurable sense of having received a bonus when, surprisingly, Dad's boss pays for the drinks. Dad expands his uncoordinated shoulders like an ungainly moth opening fully in a headlight, Mum becomes uncontrollably girlish. As she giggles the salmon frill flounces on her monumental neck.

Sitting at a white metal table, *sitting pretty*, as Dad might have put it, only a shadow of anguish, because they hadn't drunk that much. Dad's boss was getting up to go so there was no more time. They catch each other's eye, a look which says specifically, *We weren't to know.* But he might not've paid if the bill was bigger. There was always that. So all said, they'd done well, done okay. *A bird in the hand . . .* their mutual reasoning. A kind of sigh shakes out of them and they're shifting on their chairs into positions which express their comparative satisfaction at the state of things, looking soft but not too soft, calm but not unmindful.

At the moment of the shared look Josie is passing by three uniform gardens, green square of lawn, red and white border, a path. As they shift and settle she crosses in front of two concreted carports and a rose garden. What she'd really like is to find a cool kind of a place where she'd sweat less, and stink less as a consequence. A ragged frontage to one of the houses has given a tiny bit of comfort, but it's not enough and she's passed it all too soon. The rest of the gardens in the row intimidate her with their stiffness.

Bastard, she suddenly shouts at the glossy window of a house she passes and a hiccup breaks through, and sweat pours out at twice the rate because of her fury. She wipes her forehead with one sun-baked arm.

Mum and Dad sip the remainder of their drinks, their *full English Sunday breakfasts* now digested to the point where they can take on the idea of the cold chicken that's cooked and waiting in the fridge. 'Paul,' Mum calls to her six year old who's busy right now playing round the children's' slide. He hears her but doesn't respond because what he wants is for Mum to come over and watch him climb up the steps and slide down to the bottom. In the end she and Dad go across and stand at the slide while he clambers up. Paul elbows the rest of the kids out of the way, no question. His Mum and Dad're there so he knows he can get away with it. They chuckle fondly as they see his tawny head getting higher and higher, and the heads of the other kids ducking sideways, falling back. Then he's at the summit, in the sitting position and waiting to come down, this slight pause while he beams his uncomplicated pleasure.

Josie has stopped her skidding mid zigzag, there's a good reason why. An invitation to the cool space she's been dreaming of all afternoon. Can't take her eyes off it, sweet sight of an open window. A window left open, just imagine, in this harsh unfriendly bastard of a street, unbelievable. She sniffs at the air like a fox. A keen moment. Rank red fox on the prowl. Josie for you, light fingered, eyes alive to everything under the sun, show her two inches of gap at the bottom of a window and she's there. Like now. No hesitation, she trots across, takes in the red front door closed against her, but then there's a doormat saying *Welcome*, and a bush of blue hydrangea on the step which reminds her of her granny so it's *like* an invitation. And right away she has her hands under the window frame. She keeps still a minute, listening out. Foxy. All quiet, she can go for it. The house looks dark and cool through the gauzy curtain, she has the strongest feeling it's just waiting for her, egging her on. So she's applying pressure and the window's sliding upwards. Fear and thrill of it, and she gets this surge of heart-warmth. A moment like this makes up for a lot of sorrow.

Great, oh great, she mutters half under breath. Gift from heaven this open window. She feels special, favoured by unseen powers.

Paul walking on air between his mum and dad, leaning on a hand of each, a few paces then down. *Again*, he calls and up he goes, feet twiddling, forwards and back, forwards and back, like a shaky skater. He dreams of a row of fish fingers with a mound of chips to the left and a round pile of peas to the right, no, beans. Green image gone to orange, spreading orange. Better. Golden, yellow and orange, his fave. He adds half a tomato then takes it away, doesn't really like tomatoes so why have it. Milkshake, a milkshake ud be good. In the fantasy he can't decide between banana or strawberry. He wonders if there'll be a real milkshake for tea, there is on special days. Mum and Dad had those pale brown drinks in tall glasses so maybe it *is* a special day. There'd been slices of cucumber stuck on the rims of the glasses. *That* was special. It must mean a milkshake is to come. Chocolate. He remembers chocolate's best.

Driving home in the too-hot afternoon. Mum opens a window but it seems as if there's no air anywhere. She fans her face with her hand picturing the prepared food in the fridge. Cold chicken, salad in the glass dish with cling film to keep it fresh.

'Mum, can we have spaghetti hoops?' Paul's voice with a question which reinforces her sense of stability. Familiar and answerable.

'Can I have a milkshake?'

She fans slowly, gives her son a smile with a suggestion of *yes* about it.

Back in time for lunch. Food's prepared, table's lying ready. Three place mats, three knives and forks—the smallest, child's ones, for Paul. The fruit patterned plates, the placemats, waiting in a row. Knife fork spoon, knife fork spoon, knife fork spoon, she sighs with comfort. Side plates, glass tumblers, accoutrements absolutely Sunday.

Josie's red lonely face has screwed itself into a smile unusually radiant. She's at this moment trying out all the chairs at the table and settling for the smallest—a chair with no responsibility. So sweet this little chair, making her want to say *Ahh,* but it gives way under her weight, next minute she's on the soft carpeted floor. Then she's up, and off to the kitchen, scavenging, tearing off strips from this cooked chicken she's come across, dipping them into hot mustard, ketchup. Makes her wince when she swallows. So it's a spoon of jam to take the taste away and a shake of milkshake powder across her tongue. Sweet powder which she licks in. She pours a little mound of powder onto a cupboard top where it mixes with some milk she's already spilt there. The milk seeps in, the powder whitish turning yellow, looks like a mess of wet sand, she sticks out her tongue as though to just lap up the lot of it. And she can't help laughing because, this is Fun. Fun. Takes her mind off things she wants to forget about like where's she gonna stay tonight, how's she gonna get some money together and that. She just laughs, because she needs this release from the horror of life's burdens she can't really ever escape from. Fun! Honey, mustard, jam. Piece of cake, biscuit from some tin. Oh its great this, great. It's the crazy freedoms she always wants to be having. This is what life *should* be. Chicken, beer, the lot. She treads crumbs into the floor heavily, feeling good about creating the mess. Being here, mingling and making a difference, making her mark. Bathroom next. Josie's in there experimenting with toothpaste, soap and hair gel. Swigging beers, running both the taps at full. All the essences she can find she's tipped into the water and it's high peaked now with stiff white foam. What a state of ecstasy she's in. All this stuff everywhere to squander, all this possibility. And she shits on the floor daubing traces of her own excrement on white and blue windmill tiles. Rushing up to the wall in a frenzy which is almost blind. It started off as love but was quickly contaminated by rage and pain. Josie. Here she goes, her hand working fast. Up and down the wall, round and round without stopping. Smearing, smearing and working the brown malleable paste with her hands. The smell gets to her once or twice, she'll retch, then forget about it, carry on. Torment of offering followed by release. She stands still stares at her handicraft, her body leaning forward as she lets out fast breath. Then she's had enough and goes off in search of bedrooms and the right bed in which to sink herself without fear.

The street, two trees on the corner, one horse chestnut, one lime, rows of gardens. Three small lawns surrounded with almost identical flowers. The car glides along quietly. Family of three behind the glass. The one straggly garden. Three pairs of eyes skim over it without seeing, according to habit. As Josie snuggles into the boy's tiny bed and snores into his *Thomas Tank* pillowcase, the car passes the two car ports, the colourful rose garden and a crazy paved pink square. Nearly home. Now the bend in the road from where they can see the distant outline of their own front door, dark studded and glistening, imposing, like the door to some fortress. Now they're drawing up. Hydrangea, the doorstep, doormat with *welcome* etched into the bristle.

Josie dreams and dribbles, lets out her beery breath in rasps which sound like happiness. It's mid afternoon, a mature heat, the bedroom in which she sleeps is close. The pavement outside is still white in the glare, there's no wind at all. Dad stands by the front gate his eyes gone dark and squinty, Mum's behind him with Paul. Then Paul's moved in front. There's something up, he senses it in his father's lifted head. 'What's going on?' he asks Dad, sounding in that moment strangely *like* his dad.

'I don't know, son,' says Dad looking grave.

'Is there somebody in our house Dad?' Paul whispers quietly, as though to protect Mum's ears from the disturbing thought. But that very moment Mum lets out a scream. Dad is grim faced, Paul is frightened. The front window's wide open and the bottom of the net curtain is sticking out, caught against the brickwork like a distended tongue.

'Oh my God,' Mum shrieks, making Paul grip Dad's hand tightly.

'Shh,' says Dad to Mum. They stand at the gate in a ring of tight silence. The minute forms and passes.

'Shall we call the police?' Mum asks Dad.

'I reckon whoever broke in has already gone.'

They stand and listen. No sound.

Dad unlocks the front door and goes in. 'Will you look at this Beryl,' he calls back, using Mum's actual name in the drama of the moment.

Mum goes and looks. What she sees is the fridge door standing open and trails of milk and powder streaked across the floor.

A couple of beer bottles lie sideways in a pool of brownish liquid. 'How disgusting!' Mum says angrily.

Paul squeezes through the doorway. 'Who did it?'

'That's what I'd like to find out,' says Dad grimly.

Paul, less frightened now because nobody's there says, 'How can we get em?'

In the dining room the sight of Paul's chair lying on its side with one of the struts snapped brings a tear to Mum's eye. 'What vile people there are in this world.'

Dad's heart burns white with rage.

'What's that?' Mum asks suddenly. They all look upwards towards the ceiling. It's Josie's snores they can hear. Without another word the three of them move solidly to the stairs. Going upwards with a shuffle and a creak. Stone-like thudding and pad of their feet, eyes stare forward as though in some trance. At Paul's bedroom door they stop. There's a break in Josie's breathing pattern, she grunts, rolls over in the bed arms flailing, her head thrashing against the pillow. The action brings them to life.

Paul's crying. 'She's in my bed,' he keeps on saying as he stares at her strands of grease-gold hair flung out across the red and green smiles of Thomas Tank.

Mum shrieks out, 'You filthy bitch,' and Dad rushes forward grunting inarticulately his face unevenly red like a pomegranate.

Josie's awake now and she's leaping up into the air in her blue jeans and sweaty underwired black lace bra. She grabs at her tee-shirt as she moves.

'Get your eyes off my tits,' she yells at Dad. 'Dirty bastard,' she's shouting as she gets hold of her boots by the bed. She's scared but fast. In a minute she's up and rushing past them, leaping, jumping down the stairs, practically falling. But she makes it to the sitting room, goes straight for the open window and springs through it like a cat.

One second's quiet then the family rushes to the front upstairs window, see Josie flying down the street beyond the hedge, gold stranded hair streaking out behind her. Mum shudders. 'I feel all unclean, coming into contact with that horrible . . . . .' her voice breaks down altogether and she starts to sob, her massive shoulders heaving to the rhythm. Acute distress.

'I'm going to have a bath,' she splutters.

'I'm calling the police,' Dad says sternly. 'And I'm having security panels fitted to those windows.'

Boozy Josie still running, going wildly, not knowing where, tears that have collected in the corners of her eyes squirting out. She's frightened, yes, but, there's this deeper feeling building, satisfaction, a timid triumph. As if she's trickled herself across forbidden stones and left her stain there and can't be washed away, will *never* be, no matter how they scrub and scour and try to forget. An indelible mark. A smile starts to spread itself through her face understanding this, because it means *everything* to her to be blended in, to be *connected*. Suddenly she's having the awareness very strongly that she's finally broken through.

Salamander

Nerine's brother Stephen, walking out into the garden, seeing everything sleek silver with rain, coming out of the tiny doorway of that house they shared, seeing Nerine sitting on a stone by the pool, seeing a salamander run across her legs. He called her *Salamander* then forever after, because of the way her quick head would dart, her quick words would come. This incident opened his eyes to her. There was no other name that really said enough about her speed and her lightness and the bright flare of her smile. *Salamander.* It was the best time for Nerine, the time of the genesis of her new name.

When Stephen fell in love with his twin sister Babe, the bright one—Nerine the salamander, was left in the cold. She was thrown out, or walked out, one early winter morning to fend for herself, yes, things had come to that. And Nerine had fended. She had a practical disposition and an inkling she could be a nurse.

This is a story about how there *was* a brother even though Juanita, and Don, who knew her later, hadn't thought so; they assumed she'd imagined there was one. They did not believe he really existed, and then there he was on the doorstep with a shopping bag. It is also about how Nerine was burdened. Her life was oppressed by troublesome small things that bit into her, reducing her to something much less than she might have been. Her life it seems, was a battle that she couldn't win. Nerine went about in a distracted and agitated manner as if she wanted to be, or ought to be, totally somewhere else, longing for a past which perhaps had never happened, a future which couldn't be. The past and the future encroached heavily on the now, robbing Nerine of the best part of it. There was just a little sliver of now left, it leapt and bounded across her lap surprising people, it was there in her smile.

Juanita and Don are the neighbours who witness Nerine's anxious comings and goings. She's not one to linger in the hallway though she'll talk soon enough and tell them things when they are there with her face-to-face, but Juanita has seen Nerine in the swimming pool in the early evenings, when she's on her morning shift. She's always doing the breaststroke, putting in a lot of energy but not getting very far. Somehow, although this is a pool and not the sea, Nerine is going against the tide. Nerine, all at sea in the swimming pool, floundering in the ripples made by stronger swimmers. She's in up to the neck but her head's held high. It seems she is a swimmer who doesn't want to get her hair wet, her short boy's-look hair, which is slick with spray anyway so she really needn't have bothered—her fringe is plastered to her eyebrows. But maybe it's her face she wants to keep dry. There's a look of constant battle about Nerine wherever she is, she has the appearance of someone who has to fight every inch of the way forward. It's wearing her out but she won't give in. When passing swimmers flip water droplets across her she has an unforgiving look that she carries with her until she leaves. But by the time Juanita has noticed this she and Nerine are no longer speaking. Juanita dates this from the time Nerine came round one night to borrow a candle and saw Don in Juanita's bed.

Nerine is ridiculously juvenile, she must be forty, Juanita says. Don is the one who has to hear the details of their silence.

He sees Nerine quite a bit, on the off chance, her distracted face always breaking into an unexpectedly charming smile. At these moments she certainly doesn't seem like someone who would bear malice towards anybody; that smile convinces him completely it's Juanita who's the one to blame. On Saturdays he often sees her coming back from the Farmers' Market and they stop and have a little chat. She'll tell him about her electricity bills and the overcharging, and the muddle the Housing Association has made with her rent for the third month running, and her water rates, how she's paying off what they say she still owes at her former flat, and she shouldn't be. She has to go and get legal help again. Nerine, her short legs awkward in their green wellie-boots, looking up towards the sky as if she's expecting rain. Her wool skirt shifts in the wind, pleats puce and heather, recalling a country life far from here. There's a wavy blue plastic slide in her hair suggesting water, making her look childish. Don pictures the buckets and spades of a child's seaside holidays. A simple life without worry that she can't yet find again though she's hoping to. The brother has moved to Canada, he has bought a house; Nerine is waiting to join him. *It is miles from anywhere,* Nerine says complacently. Don nods and smiles at her. At this time he doesn't believe there really is a brother. He, like Juanita, thinks Nerine has made him up.

But why would she? Either he or Juanita has said at least a hundred times. This is the preamble to their discussion of the why's and wherefores.

The brother is her carapace, Juanita once remarked and Don, having thought it through found this apt. The brother gave hope to Nerine's life and supplied her with a need to buy little treasures. These she stored up in boxes that she stood around her bedroom. Over time she had to move out of the bedroom as the boxes filled up all of the space. From floor to ceiling there wasn't anything else. Nerine moved into the living room. Here too, after a while, boxes lined the walls. There was enough space in the middle for a couch,—which Nerine also used as a bed—a fridge, a small table and a microwave. Her TV was fixed on a ledge high up near the ceiling and didn't take up any ground space. Nerine went to markets and bargain basements and antique shops and she bought her treasures. She looked at them and then put them in a box. Evenings she spent getting out a box or two at random and sorting through her things. She displayed them on the small table taking care to keep them away from the sauce bottles and the butter; she held them up to the bit of light that managed to get in there through the drab mottled curtain. They were more entertaining than anything the TV had to offer.

It must give her comfort to be surrounded by all these treasures, Juanita said with a shrug. *If there were no brother whose house she was expecting to move to, she'd have no reason to buy the stuff.*

Don had the flat next to Nerine. There was never a sound coming from her place. He seldom knew if she was in or on duty at the hospital. Until that moment when he'd see her in the hallway or out on the street, rushing along with a new treasure—to get it safely boxed, he guessed, as soon as possible—it was as if she didn't really exist. If he hadn't actually stopped and talked to her she'd have been gone in a flash, in and out of shadow, somewhere and then nowhere so fast he'd have been left wondering if he'd really seen her. Her face, of course, would be twisted up with anxiety over something or another. Nerine was hounded by her troubles even in flight.

She wants to pretend I'm not here. She tries to unthink me, I can see that. And so I play along, is what Nerine says to Don when he meets her by chance coming into the building.

But you and Juanita used to be such friends, Don tells her, to which she gives a snort, or makes a sound very like a snort. This is her only reply.

Didn't you, Don says, to draw out something more specific.

Nerine is staring out across the narrow communal garden. And when she speaks she repeats, *so I play along with her. That's what you have to do in such cases.*

And now you're not on speaking terms. Don looks at Nerine closely, sees her eyes have become intense.

I can't speak to Juanita, Nerine says, her voice confidential. *You see, she's mad. She's mad and she wants me out of here. It's as simple as that. There are cases like that at the hospital. But I'm strong from dealing with the mad people there. I know how to deal with her. What I do, whenever I bump into her is to pretend I don't really exist. You know, with mad people, it can be dangerous to make any kind of eye contact. Juanita would like to break me but she won't. I'm playing her game you see, I'm letting her think I'm not here after all. I'm ignoring her because it makes me safe, not because I want to.*

Don can't pretend he's not shocked at hearing this stuff. Juanita and he are close after all, now and again they're even lovers, though with no commitment as they're both recovering from long term relationships and can't take anything more substantial. But it's not that they don't like one another. Don knows he's frowning. He'd walk right on but there's this bit of him that wants to find out more.

You don't believe me, Nerine says quietly. *And I'm not surprised because Juanita is a good actress. She keeps her true self well hidden.*

Don thinks the best thing to do is to act very calmly or he'll never be able to get to what's really behind all this. *But, why would Juanita want you out of here, Nerine?*

Nerine considers Don's question. He thinks he sees a crafty look creep into her eyes. *I can't go into that,* she tells him. *But I'll just say that sometimes these things aren't even personal. It may be nothing to do with me as such. I'm the one who just happens to be here. I'm the occasion. In the Psychiatric Wing there are a number of similar cases.* She picks up her bag that she's left resting by her feet and passes quickly on into the hall, closes the door.

Don is left to ponder this, left wondering. Not that he's really wondering. Nerine is upset about something. He leaves it at that. It's only now and again, later, when he looks at Juanita, he has the thought, malignant and unwelcome. Could she, would she? *Is* she? Then reaction sets in, guilt. A Friday night. He's spending it round at Juanita's. They're in bed by now—it's ten o'clock. He watches her across the gap of bed. A few seconds spent watching, in his heart, suspicion. Then he looks at her again. No, impossible.

Meeting Nerine on the Saturday, coming in from the Farmers' Market her bag laden with leeks and celery—his eyes catch onto their waving tops and the truth hits him. He sees Nerine for what she is, a crazy woman. She starts off at once going on about the non-existent brother. How she was just about to go to join him in the house in Canada, but then *Nine Eleven* happened and she was afraid to fly. She's still afraid to. It'll be some time yet before she'll build up the courage. Or does Don think she's wrong here? Should she go anyway? She tightens the plastic slide on its strand of hair.

He shrugs helplessly.

And then it's, maybe she should, maybe she should put the horrors out of her mind and just go for it.

He shrugs again. What to say?

But no, perhaps she'll wait.

Waiting is Nerine's style; it's her game plan. If it is a game, if she does have a plan. To wait.

Up on the diving board Juanita sees Nerine with arms stretched up. As if she's about to dive, as if she will. Sometime.

But what about her hair, what about her precious face? Juanita is thinking as she leaves the swimming pool. If Nerine dives into the water her hair and her face will get all wet. Juanita walks away from the building, goes down the street, not caring enough about what will happen to induce her to stay. What will be will be. What is, is. In her heart she carries a picture of Nerine static. She's stretching her arms up to the rafters forever. Who knows what the conclusion will be?

Nerine is with Don on the street. They are walking; she won't let him get away today until he's heard what's on her mind. She has him for a sympathetic listener. He is, but with limitations. Hearing about the hospital, how the other nurses have got it in for her is one thing, but Juanita, being told that Juanita is persecuting Nerine is a thing he really doesn't want to hear. He shifts uncomfortably in his shoes. Can't bear to hear it but keeps quiet, wants to hear more. He's pulled in the two directions.

Every night Juanita taps five times on the water pipe. She knows it will reverberate, keep me from sleeping. Somehow she waits till I'm just at the point of sleep. When she takes out her rubbish bags to the bins she drops just a little bit of shredded cabbage or rotten fish-head—a foody thing you can be sure. Drops it just near my front door, next to the mat.

Don is quick here, he's seen a flaw in Nerine's story. *I'm sure it must be an accident. You can't be saying Juanita would do such a thing on purpose. You said what Juanita wanted was for you to not exist. You said she wouldn't want to be reminded you are here. If Juanita is doing this to you it means she's aware of you. She's reminding herself. Why don't you just speak to her? Tell her to be more careful.*

I can't do that, can I, Nerine says.

I don't see why not, Don tells her curtly, as though to say Nerine has kept quiet only because she wants to prolong the bad blood of the situation.

Because, she goes. *Because. I'd be playing into her hands, wouldn't I.*

Nerine gives a wild sudden laugh, returning Don to his belief she's a little unbalanced. More than a little. He ponders this thought quietly.

Nerine continues, *The logic isn't as clear-cut as you imagine. She wants to know I don't exist but she has this compulsion to keep on testing to see if it's true. She's trying to draw me out but if I'm drawn out I'm in danger. If I don't take the bait I'm safe. But she'll keep on trying. There are many such cases in the hospital. In the psychiatric wing it's an everyday occurrence. Signs. The mad are always looking for signs.*

Don and Juanita lean together and whisper, conspiratorial with this new thought they've had lately. *Is Nerine a nurse at the hospital, or a patient? Is she, or has she at some time been a patient in the psychiatric ward.* She knows so much about the place; she knows so much about mental states. Just one subtle tweak of the facts would be all it would take. *And so?*

One Tuesday night. Don meets Nerine on the stairs. She's looking agitated, wants him to come into her place and help her shift a bucket of water. Would he mind? No, of course he wouldn't mind but where did the water come from? The pipe next to her sink is split, it's spilling water. She's called the emergency services, she's waiting for the plumber. The plumber was supposed to come last week, he was supposed to come yesterday.

How did the pipe split? Don asks her.

Old useless pipe,' Nerine spits back.

She can't shift the bucket because she's hurt her shoulder lifting a heavy patient at the hospital. Two nurses are supposed to do that job but the other nurses hate her, they all gang up on her; they made her lift the patient on her own. Now she's done something to her shoulder. She can't move it; her whole back is full of pain, as if there are a thousand splinters piercing her. Walking is difficult. She's off work now. Doesn't know if she'll ever be able to work again. She's got to try and get legal advice about compensation.

Don edges through the doorway of Nerine's flat. She's got a kitchen/living room that she uses as a bedsit. Two rows of light brown cardboard storage boxes line the walls. They are higher than when he was here last time; they have nearly reached the level of the television. In the centre of the piled boxes is an oasis of living space. A couch with a cluttered coffee table in front of it, a small fridge next to that with the microwave on the top. A rug. At the edge of the rug the boxes start, the room is not large. There's a gap and then the sink on the far wall. The bedroom door is open. That room is full of boxes, except there's a narrow corridor and this is how Nerine gets in. To inspect the contents of random boxes Don supposes.

I've made up my mind to leave, Don hears Nerine saying. *But there's a problem with my documents.* He nods, lifting up the bucket. *I have to see my solicitor.*

He hears her vaguely, isn't really listening. Nerine's constant lamentations can be a little hard to keep an enthusiasm for. He takes the bucket of water to Nerine's shower room, a sparse tiny rectangle with a single threadbare towel, a packet of bleach. How Nerine can live the way she does Don can't begin to imagine.

She's waiting, Juanita says. *She won't waste anything on the present. It's only the future and the past Nerine's got any time for. In her mind perhaps, she's already gone on to somewhere else or has never left where she used to be.*

Ten AM, a Thursday, nothing exceptional, nothing new, nothing you'd call new. Except there's this smell. Juanita in her kitchen making toast notices it. Something between grease and fireworks, she's not sure what. Don's just about to go in to work with the report he's been working on. There's a faint, sickening odour, he can't tell where it's coming from. Then half way to his door with an arm in one sleeve of his jacket, the fire alarms go off. The ones in the flats, recurrent sirens, shrill and screaming, and the one in the hallways, like a thousand clanging bells. Together and out of harmony, these two alarms rip through the building. In a few minutes Don's out on the pavement, and here's Juanita, looking sheepish.

I was just making toast, she tells him. *And now this.*

Next the fire engine arrives.

I was just making toast, Juanita says, feeling bad about it, still thinking at this moment it's her fault the alarm's gone off. *You have to make toast on the windowsill in this place. Who can do that?*

The firemen check her flat. *No, it's flat No. 3,* one of them calls, just when the investigation's nearly over. By the time they get to Nerine's, the smoke's billowing. She's not coming out, not answering. Don looks at Juanita, sees her face gone white with terror. It mirrors his feeling. They move tremblingly into the entrance porch. Don tries to get back in the building; he thinks of Nerine trapped inside her little space. But the firemen won't let him re-enter. By now they're kicking in Nerine's door, calling out. The door's down, they're going in. A smoky haze through which they see the rectangular doorway to the bedroom. It's orange with flame. No sight or sound from Nerine, no cry, not even a whisper. They fight the flame with water, spraying it down to nothing, reveal Nerine's body lying across some burned up lumpy boxes just into the room.

A shudder passes between Don and Juanita in the entrance porch, as though they too have seen her lying there crumpled and partly blackened and dried out as a twig.

When the ambulance comes Nerine is rushed to hospital. She doesn't survive, but it isn't till some time later that Don and

Juanita know this. They keep phoning the hospital and nobody can tell them anything about Nerine. The impersonal voices at the end of the line keep saying they've never heard of anybody of that name, they say she has never been admitted. It's as if they are in collusion with the kind of troubled life Nerine had had and they're determined to reproduce it. Even now the same problematic things are going on.

But she was a nurse at the hospital, Don shouts out, distraught. *No,* they say, and then the phone cuts off.

She must have been admitted, Don repeats to Juanita, his head hollow with the sense of nightmare. *She can't just have disappeared.* He phones again, reaches this department, that department, this ward, that ward, everywhere. Then he goes to the hospital in person, to make enquiries. He stands at the entrance desk. The receptionists on the other side give him confident and empty smiles, they could be robots. They check their records, eyes aloof. *No, he must be mistaken. It must be the hospital the other side of Town, Nerine—was that the name?—she must be somewhere else.* Don slips away from their blank-screen faces, tired, brought down by the weight of their denial.

That night police come round and interview Don and Juanita. They say Nerine's a missing person, ask them for a description. *But there was a fire,* Don bursts out. *Nerine left here in an ambulance.* The police seem to know nothing about this; they say they'll contact the Fire Department. Three days later Don phones the police and is told Nerine has died. Don and Juanita are in a state of shock.

And yes, she had been a nurse, yes she had died in that same hospital where she'd worked, only there had been some kind of mix up with the records. It's a sad story. She'd been taken in with burns and acute asphyxiation. The hospital when Don calls them, says who is he, is he a relative? He says he's a neighbour and they say they can't give out any information, as he isn't kin. It is like a replay of Nerine's own experience of life. The affliction, the pain. The unbelievable difficulty. Uncanny that.

Don has a mental picture of Neriné a candle in her hand as she looks at some lacy treasure, a soft bit of cloth susceptible to the flame. The flame catches. Soon to be all over with her. He pictures how Nerine dies, pictures the boxes catching light around her, her hair on fire, the hairslide melting quickly. Boxes hold her in, collapsing in front of her till she's all cut off. Boxes tumbling. She, Nerine, bright and resisting as she leaps and twists. But it's too much for her. She falls.

She leaps and twists before his eyes at unexpected moments. In the hallway, in the street at places he most frequently used to see her. Light and shadow. She, slipping in and out of them as usual. Her worried look. Hard for Don to believe at first the swift and darting Nerine does not exist, except as ashes.

Ashes in a casket in a shopping bag, let's be brutal, Juanita says.

Juanita believes such things have to be said, that reality has to be looked at harshly or it won't be taken in. Nerine who always tried to make light of the present and be there in it as little as possible was far more a thing of substance than she could have imagined or wished. For even when the harsh things are said, Don and Juanita find it hard to accept she's dead, and that's the truth of it. They stare at the shopping bag in Stephen's hand, a scarred bag of everyday leather. The sight of it is what at last convinces them. Almost without knowing it, they've been toying with a sense of the sacred, something extra terrestrial. The shopping bag has undercut its presence.

I know it's wrong to fall in love with your sister. It's a false thing, a thing not to be tolerated. This is what the brother Stephen would have liked to hear himself saying to them, if he'd been able to get the words out. Maybe Nerine hated me because I was in love with Babe. Sometimes I even hope she did hate me. I expect condemnation—I almost need it. And there's also the jealously factor. I'm talking about Nerine feeling left out. The intensity of twinship excluded her, she must have had a terrible sense of isolation. *Nerine fell out with Babe and so she left us to fend for herself. She didn't ever come back,* is all he actually does say.

But who is Babe? Don asks self-consciously, the name *Babe* embarrassing him as he shuffles out the question.

But who is Babe? Don asks self-consciously, the name *Babe* embarrassing him as he shuffles out the question.

Don as if falling from a great height. Things flashing past his eyes as he goes. This bit of the past, that bit, all bringing him right down to the present. He can't remember the last time he'd seen Nerine. He thinks of the fire, again imagines the boxes alight, those same boxes he'd seen in their dull brown ordinary state. He'd almost felt the rough texture of the cardboard when Nerine had absently run her fingers across the ones next to the sink. The day he'd gone to carry away the bucket of water seems far off and close, in equal measures. A small action, strange he'd noticed it at all. Nothing significant, except it spelled the feeling of life and now here's the opposite. Ashes. Do ashes *feel?* He laughs in spite of his misery. All the unresolved troubles. Don shakes his head as if to dispel them. Nerine never managed it, more's the pity. They'll have to be dispelled, now. He thinks of the faded look of her curtain, of the TV high on the wall with its own waiting look. The smile of Nerine, its surprising lively quality.

The police have been and gone. And now on the doorstep is Stephen, the brother. In his mind he says, Wrongly I fell in love with Babe my twin sister, also known as Caroline. All passed smoothly until the day Nerine saw Caroline and me lying together in the long grass. The wind whooshed the grass apart and there we were. My fault. No, not just the carelessness. Of course it was my fault. It shouldn't have been happening. Me and Babe, we shouldn't have been as we were, but there was this terrible pull between us. Twinship. Nerine couldn't handle it, and why should she? You could call it incest. But it felt like a love I'd never get over. In the end Caroline left me. She married five years ago and went to live in Wales. I've never visited. No, it's never seemed the right thing. I live by myself now, very quietly. I had hoped Nerine would join me. I have a house. It would have been just the two of us. Not that I mean to say . . . No, it's not at all like that. Why didn't she come? She must have been lonely living by herself in that pokey flat. Why couldn't she be more forgiving? After all that time you'd think she could have let go of what she'd seen. You'd think she could have got past it.

Stephen says, *Babe was what we used to call my twin sister. I don't know why, her name is Caroline. Nerine was the baby of the family, if anybody was.*

I hoped she'd come out and join me, but Nerine always loved to play a waiting game. Maybe she would have come one day, we can never know. She fell out with Babe and left one frosty morning. And now this. I'm never going to see Nerine again. He looks at the shopping bag, thinks of Nerine reduced to a little pot of ashes that have to be carried in a bag for the sake of public acceptability. The myth he's had of Nerine has given him a sense of security, a something allegorical about her that has always soothed him. He'd been working on the assumption she was imperishable. He cries.

Don and Juanita on the step, both with an arm around Stephen. They invite him in for coffee, both eyeing the shopping bag uneasily at the same time. But no, he'll be going, he guesses, he's staying in a hotel the other side of town. He'll be back tomorrow to sort through Nerine's things – if there is anything left which hasn't been burnt.

So what was she waiting for? Don's voice sounds hopeless. *What?* He'd like things to be different; he'd like Nerine to have found whatever it was. *But then again maybe she wasn't waiting for anything and it was just an act. Or it seemed like waiting to everyone else. Maybe Nerine's pride wanted people to go along with thinking there were other options she could take if she wanted to. But it was possible there wasn't anything she could go on to after all. Nothing she felt right about.*

Juanita says, *Nerine saw us together once. The door swung open unexpectedly. Just a couple of seconds, but she saw you lying in my bed. It might have shocked her, Nerine was hardly adult, was she? — I mean did you ever know her to have a relationship even?* She pauses. *It was one night when her electricity had broken down. It kept on breaking down didn't it, if you remember. She came to borrow a candle.*

A candle? Don says unhappily. *Don't.*

It was round about that time I sensed hostility coming from her. Not long after, we even stopped speaking.

Juanita thinking of Nerine up on the diving board, or slowly making her way through the swimming pool. Nerine in water but not succumbing, never giving in to it. Nerine with her arms outstretched as if reaching out for other possibilities. Stuck in the past and waiting for the future to happen.

And the brother goes on his way in the next day or two, goes back to Canada, thinking how myths, though deep and universal, can be deeply and universally fallible. You can't rely on them. Who could withstand such a fire! No mortal creature, no salamander even. Where did this idea come from that a salamander could not burn? He himself was guilty of believing Nerine was protected in some strange way by something bigger than all of them, by the charisma of some reified glory, by perfection, a story larger than words. But he knows now Nerine was just a woman. It's a lesson that is painfully difficult to learn.

Tango

The white and turquoise Hotel Esplanade at 7 am. A Tuesday. Chipolatas, scrambled egg, grilled tomato halves. This is always the breakfast on a Tuesday. Served with triangles of toast. The breakfast waitress is now in her fifth season here and it hasn't varied in that time. She is at this moment in the dining room laying out breakfast cups. Mint green with a dark foresty motif. She is feeling low. She has felt low at about this time every morning for five years. Placing a grey steel teaspoon in each laid out saucer she begins to sigh.

This year's summer receptionist has just come in and has given the breakfast waitress her customary unsympathetic small stare. Already she has transferred her attention to the cover of her bright glossy magazine. She sits with her legs sideways resting together at the knees and brings her long-stay gloss coated lips into a line which is part disapproval of the breakfast waitress's frowsty complexion, part relish for the contents of the fast-set mag.

At 7.15 the breakfast waitress shoves her hair roughly from her face, dragging it back as far as possible as though to punish it for being greasy. She scrapes at her pulpy cheeks with vigour to get rid of any strands that are hanging about there, and then, when it's all done, she begins to moan. The moans start off quietly but become quite loud, and *gluggy*, as though she's building up to tears.

Oh no, don't let her start crying now, anything but that. The receptionist almost prays this, as it is she's forced to hold her hands over both her ears to block out the racket. But no, actual tears are held off, there's a final moaning crescendo and then silence.

The receptionist has turned her shoulder far enough round to make sure she won't catch sight of the grey-flabby resentful face of the waitress even if she happens to look up by accident. She draws on her skill of special instant deafness to keep herself untainted by the antics of *the madhouse*, as she calls this place.

It has turned 7.30. The breakfast waitress, now purged of her bitter humours starts to pick up a bit. She's beginning to appreciate the sight of the half laid table, the collections of sauce bottles on the sideboard in two columns, brown and red, the fresh sun of the morning. Now something else is happening to her face. Her rather narrow features are broadening, softening, and at last a smile spreads its way across her mouth. The pulpy look is gone, she's all aglow. The receptionist breathes more freely and doesn't mind if she does catch Rose's eye, knowing the awful morning anguish has played itself out.

The sun is bright now. It streaks against the windows of the Hotel Esplanade, lights up the dining room. The white and turquoise exterior, designed to ward off suspicions about seediness, reveals meandering cracks, patches of mould, dust, all those signs of decay resented by Bella the receptionist as a slur against her perfect finish.

By now it's 8 o clock. The breakfast waitress has put out a place mat depicting an Irish castle, a plate to the left, a cup and saucer, cup face down, to the right, and a knife and fork always the same space apart, many times. The exactness and the routine comfort her. Sight of the uniformity, such a pleasure. She stands back, surveys the sea of tables, all decked out neatly this way. At this moment, so close to happiness, it becomes possible for her Rose, to actually smile at Bella, the receptionist, and know by instinct the smile won't be rejected. It won't be, because the two women are in harmony for the first time this morning. Bella too is comforted by the sight of the laid tables and has begun to feel warmer towards Rose.

'Would you get me a coffee please, Rosie,' Bella asks rather than orders, looking at her watch. And Rose, who loves to be needed flies away to the kitchen feeling almost optimistic. It's her best time of day, this. Up to this point it's always a nightmare beginning with the chaos and rows at home, the struggle to get to the hotel on time. It's certainly true that the bright part of the day is opened by the completion of the table laying routine and then it'll go on, unless there's a glitch, and see her through the rest of the morning till the tables have been cleared away again. And during this whole good-time Rose does not fear or resent the sight of the pearlwhite fingernails, the smooth lipsticked mouth and the unfuzzy line of Bella's lightly curved eyebrows. She feels easy about everything.

Rose brings Bella's coffee *nicely* on a 50's baroque tea tray. *With lilies*, she thinks, admiring the heavy peach flowers embossed on the side of the cup. Rose smiles appreciatively as the ornate tray is placed on the table beside her.

At 8.15 everything is ready. Packets of cereal stand grouped together on the sideboard, the orange juice cartons have been satisfyingly snipped and the juice poured with a gush into three glass jugs, sauce bottle tops have been wiped. Rose and Bella are standing side by side at the top end of the long dining room.

Bella turns to face Rose. 'Shall we?' she says.

Rose's face is all animation now, a twitch and flurry of fast smiles. 'Well, yes.'

The two women face one another, join hands and begin to dance. Round and round they go, weaving between the little square tables. Rose tips her head far back and extends her right arm. 'Cool,' says Bella and they sail away across the floor of the dining room like a fully rigged ketch venturing across a rocky sea. Their clasped hands point forward, knees are bent then straightened in unison. They manoeuvre delicately between the laid out tables and glide on past the big plate windows. They see the sun, the surging and retreating sea all a sparkle, the foreground band of red and white geraniums in the promenade gardens. Fiery crimson and gleaming white dazzling them to high heaven. On and on and out of sight.

'May it never end,' Rose whispers her face flushed now, with the shine of the moment.

Back they go towards the sideboard and the door, then away. Heads lowered, heads high, hearts bursting. A symmetrical weaving and bending and run. Flowing with the tide, out there and always like an eternal breath. Their sense of this. Again past the smudged windows hemmed in by cracked paint frames which they do not notice. Two pairs of eyes staring out as they go. A blur of sunshine, of blue, of white and crimson flower heads.

'One more time?' says Bella.

'One more time,' says Rose.

Chicken eye

Nadia's having a bit of trouble with her tongue. It's everywhere and nowhere. Sounds come, not words mind, sounds, *Shlurgh, shurralah, sphlug.* Her tongue bucks madly, awkwardly, behind her teeth, a wild horse in a too small space, still no words. And her eyes are popping as if there's this immense pressure from her insides. Twin milky-shiny globes, a fervent look to them. Yet she always has this sealed up feeling about her, Nadia, as if she's covering something up she doesn't want you to see. Frantic and bursting, but keeping a lid on it, that's Nadia. At last words *do* come, cat hasn't got her poor lolloping horse of a tongue then, she's managed, she usually does, somehow or other. Slow, ponderous words, as though the horse has run out of steam, is going back quietly into its stable. But what a build up for, *It's a nice day.* All drawled and stylised though, to make up for lack of content, that'll be Nadia's pride. And she's hugging her cushion, not a good sign. It means she's feeling insecure because of the cousins.

With her eyes she's good at trying to remind me of things we never say out loud when it's only the two of us, like that she once tried to kill herself, that she was once committed to a *mental institution.* These worst-things she'll carry like a kind of banner in her eyes, determined letters on ovoid silk. You *can't* forget, she'll never allow it, her not so hidden thought is, 'I *am* mad, maybe I am mad.' And she needs to share it, just has to keep the idea alive. She's known me all my life, and she only has to jog me along with her stares and pauses, it's enough.

Or *Tam* she'll go, with this certain kind of wavery note in her voice, and I'll know just by hearing her what she's on about. I have this feeling that being mad is a concept she's invested in, in a funny kind of way she's safe with it, forget it and where would she be? It's a question of her self identity, Nadia would go to pieces if she had to start working on a new one. As things are she's all held together nice and known. Of course if you were to say she was crazy she'd be on her high horse right away her eyes gone smudgy grey, her mouth bunched up and lumpy with regret. No, it can't be said, it must be just known in a way which doesn't need saying. *Shurrallagh.* As I say, this is if it's just the two of us, but we have the cousin strangers here. It's all completely different, she'll want them to know the things she's been through, and it'll be me who will have to be her sort of mouthpiece. They'll look from me to her nervously, say something like, 'Tut tut, good thing you're better now.' Voices sweet as honey, to soothe and settle. It won't work because she'll need to show them how things are with her, she will want to reach them.

Nadia sits with her cushion on her knee. It is coarse and black, a kind of linen texture, with a frill around it, but the front is done in appliqué, all narrow sewn-on strips in green, maroon and blue which spiral round and round like a maze in a child's puzzle book ending in a single indented mirrorwork eye. *Nadia* says it is an eye. This moment she is tracing the green strip of cloth with her finger to see if she can reach it. It's easy to get lost on the way. Nadia's my sister, she's fifteen years older than me and we've shared a house together since my parents died. I'm twenty five, I am divorced—and Nadia was married once, but that was years ago. Bill and Tina, the cousins, are from New Zealand, they don't really know us.

Nadia is unsettled, her tongue is wild with possibility, lips moving as though there are words somewhere, not quite here yet but on their way. She's limbering up for the revelations, preparing herself even though it's me who'll be saying what there is to say, to make these cousins see her the way she wants to be seen. Only when this has been accomplished can we get back to the world of quiet reminders. I hope they see things quickly, I hope they understand.

Bill and Tina wanted somewhere to stay from time to time while they're over here, they wrote and asked us. We *do* have the space. I said yes, but told them Nadia wasn't used to people. In return they're prepared to try and draw her out, to get to know us. This, in the abstract, is their idea, but I think they're used to being as solitary as we are, they might not manage it. Bill's the cousin, distant, and Tina's his wife, both sandy looking people with sharply turned up noses. Unusual. It makes Nadia laugh on sight. I can hear her tongue going at full speed, whirring as if it's a winged creature she has there in her mouth. 'Whrrr.' I glance at her but no good, of course, Nadia can't take any kind of hint.

They are very smiley when they arrive and they hug both Nadia and me, but I get the feeling they will smile and hug as much as they think necessary to fulfill their obligation as relation-strangers and no more. I also suspect they will end up smiling less than they'd intended and may not invite us for a return visit.

Bill is very freckled, Tina is not, later on I discover it's just that she's wearing foundation. At breakfast they are both freckly together, and Nadia, who can be very childish is just completely taken over by the fact they're so identical, squinting and blinking at the two of them as though they're a pair of cute matching dolls.

'Whrrr.' Nadia's whirring her head off. She's gone limp with laughter, her shoulders shake and roll. The cousins look at her with polite question marks forming.

Nadia has a habit of impersonating the quirky behaviour of whoever she is talking to. Maybe they'll be squinting, or drawing in breath in sharp little gulps. Whatever she sees she'll reproduce. I think she does it because she wants to share in their life experience. It's a kind of homage to other people and their traits. She wants to please them, make them feel at home by seeing what is familiar. People quickly come to see that Nadia's a bit *funny in the head* and so they'll play along with her, or pretend not to notice she's copying what they're doing. But there's always the danger Nadia will get upset if she thinks they're trying to humour her, or if they're ignoring her because they don't like the way she is. The *Whrrr* will be replaced by a *Srrr*, a something close to tears. Bill has this way of picking his nose and disguising it. He'll either jab his forefinger up his nostril with a vacant look to him as though it's just arbitrary the finger is where it is, or he'll do one of his elaborate tricks like suddenly staring at a place the other side of the room to make you look there, and in that moment when you are looking away, wham, he'll be doing it. Tina smells her armpits in a compulsive way, lifting one arm up as though stretching, then the other, with a sharp turn of her head to each in turn. This routine will be going on while you are at the table, during dinner say. Or sometimes she'll tap at one armpit with her finger, and she'll hold that finger out, keeping it consciously separate till she's smelt it. Maybe she's checking if the deodorant is working. She also makes sounds of agreement with what you might be saying by doing a kind of ghostly whistling noise that is partly throaty partly nasal, it's hard to say exactly how she does it. All of these traits plus others, Nadia is into almost after the first evening. It is truly amazing to see how they are able to ignore her reconstructions, and I can't help wondering if they've noticed, or even whether they're conscious of how they themselves are the models for her behaviour. I hope Nadia won't start getting agitated.

After dinner we sit around, Bill and Tina chatting to me about their day, Nadia on the two-seater couch as always, looking a bit strained, hugging her cushion. At first there's the odd bit of *whirring* from her when she pauses to consider the cousins, sometimes a sly finger in her nose, a surreptitious sniff of one of her armpits, which I ignore and they don't appear to see, then this urgency starts building in her, which I understand as the sign for me to tell the cousins about her *history*. 'Something very terrible happened to Nadia,' I say. 'A long time ago it was, when she was just eighteen.' This is the way she likes me to begin. I see Nadia's head nodding as I speak, see her settling back into the couch as though for a familiar night-time story, the cousins are silent and grave, not quite sure I ought to tell.

'Nadia was married at seventeen and soon she was going to have a baby, but there was an accident. One day, Nadia and Tony—Tony is the name of Nadia's husband—were going for a ride on his motorbike when they had to swerve to avoid a car driving on the wrong side of the road. Nadia fell off at once. She got thrown up into the air and landed on the grass verge but Tony went on down the road with the bike, skidding and buckling and finally ending up underneath it. He hit his head hard on the road and his limbs were crushed by the weight of the bike so that later when they'd got him to hospital, he died. Nadia had a miscarriage.' I have to say all this in a clear and informative way, without biting my lip or showing any other emotion, or Nadia won't be able to handle it, or maybe the truth is that I won't be able to. Well anyway this is the way I tell the story.

The cousins say they are so sorry, Nadia nods her head at them, accepting sympathy then looks at me. The story I've just told is the one I'd heard from my parents while I was growing up but there's more to tell, and this part of the story is really made up by me. I started telling the story of Nadia's suicide attempt to friends who came home from school to tea. They wanted to *know* about Nadia, what was wrong with her. The funny thing was Nadia liked to be in on the telling. I'd be directed by her smiles or frowns, her rapid shakes of the head, her nods, and over time the things I said turned into a proper story with a beginning, middle and end. The beginning was when Nadia was lying on the grass verge by the road. 'She stared out into a tangle of twigs and brambles without knowing what they were or where she was. At last she could make out the black outlines with the sky between them, she could see the grass. There was a violent pain inside her, she moved slightly, realised her legs were sticky and wet. She thought of dark red blood, she thought she would lose the baby.' The cousins look uneasy because of the details. But also they're probably having the same thought some of the school friends used to have. *Was this tragedy the cause of Nadia being the way she was or had she always been, well, mad?* The answer to this is that I don't know. I was too young to remember anything, and I just have this one memory of Nadia and Tony in black leather jackets standing in the road outside the house and perhaps that's just a fantasy.

'Our parents used to lock Nadia in her bedroom after the accident because she said she was going out to throw herself under a car. They didn't know what else to do, they said, and then they told her if she didn't stop it she'd have to be put away.' I use words that I can imagine my parents having used, these words seem to suit Nadia, she is nodding vigorously. Tina says surely she could have been prescribed tranquillizers to get her through a difficult time., or therapy. Nadia needed a good therapist. Nadia stamps a foot on the floor, pulls at the threads of her cushion. How can I tell Tina this is a *story,* that I don't know the *real* truth of what went on? I shrug.

'Nadia climbed out onto the window ledge,' I continue. 'It was quite high up, she could see cars rushing up and down on the road below, and then a crowd of people all standing together on the pavement. She screamed out and said she was going to jump, and she told them it was because of the voice of the baby. It was the lost-baby that was telling her, it crept into her bed at night and told her how she was to kill herself. Then an ambulance came and took Nadia away and she had to stay in hospital for a long time, for months, but the dead baby had found out where she was and used to come up to the window and stare in at her, stare in without blinking, stare through the shiny glass.

'In the end Nadia got better and she went home, she didn't hear the baby's voice any more or see it looking at her, but the trouble was, she missed it. She wanted to hear the voice but she never did, she tried to listen out for the sound but it never came back to her. *You are better,* the doctor and her parents and everyone said, but this did not make her happy. Most of all she wanted to see the baby at the window looking in so they'd know where each other were.'

Bill and Tina look distressed. 'It's a good thing that you're better now Dear,' Bill says for both of them. 'Thank you,' says Nadia back, then promptly follows this up with standing on her head. She's good at standing on her head is Nadia, can keep it going for hours. She *does*. We just talk round her, I am used to things like this, I guide them with my seriousness. 'There are some very good walks round here,' I say, going to get the local maps. Tina makes the whistling noise.

Nadia's cushion has been around for years, but the colours always seem to stay bright. I don't know where it came from, she got it during the time I was away from home. I came back and it was here, it's quite striking. No one else is allowed to touch it, but there was that one occasion, when our mother died six months after our father. Unlike *his* death hers was unexpected and I was so out of my mind with grief I didn't know how I'd recover. I went to bed the night after her funeral so emotionally exhausted that I finally did drift into sleep. In the morning, before I'd woken up, when I was *half awake*, I could feel this strange rough texture next to my face. It didn't feel like a pillow, it didn't feel at all right. It was Nadia's cushion, she'd put it under my head in the night to comfort me. When I got up my face was all rivets of red, and I'm sitting there and looking at it with a kind of smile even though I feel all horrible, and in comes Nadia trying to be quiet, but clumsy the way she is and rattling the door handle, with a cup of tea for me. She hadn't boiled the water and cold hard little tea leaves floated on the surface of creamish fawn. It made me cry somehow, thinking of how kind Nadia could be but how useless, and once I'd started there was no stopping. My hands were shaking heavily and Nadia took the cup away and put it on the cupboard and we sat on the side of my bed together, with her rocking me, just rocking and rocking me in her arms. In between my sobs Nadia's whispering to me that the picture on the cushion is of a chicken and all the sewn on strips are the outlines of its feathered body coiling round and round. And also they're all the dark twining branches of a bush and this bush is hiding parts of the chicken so that you cannot see everything, but the chicken sees *you*. It is always looking out from feathers and twigs and it sees you, and anything you could name. Even the dead baby, the chicken eye can see. *Just think of that.* I remember staring at the pattern and really trying to see things in there I hadn't seen before but it wasn't happening for me.

'Oh I thought it was just a pattern,' I told Nadia in my jerky, sobby voice, the very idea of this making her sigh.

When Nadia's on edge she has a washing up fetish that can be hard to take. She just can't keep herself away from the cups and the saucers and the sink. The really laughable thing is that when she's *doing the dishes* as she calls it, she's completely seri-ous, acting as though her behaviour is perfectly normal for once, and nothing *nutty* about it. *Whereas!* If you say anything she'll give you a look, as though to say she is only doing what *normal* people do, isn't she, what's the matter with that? Today she's been at the sink for half an hour with one cup and saucer, a couple of plates. She's scrubbing and scrubbing at the han-dle of the cup and probably there was no grime on it to start with, and there's this intense look on her face, it's worrying. I don't say anything but start laying the table for breakfast. The cousins come in and I just know things are going to be difficult. They're off today, touring in Scotland for a week then seeing some friends in Manchester before coming back to us and I can sense that Nadia will be unable to let them go without some serious demonstrations of her mental state. She's been talking quite a lot for her, up until now, but suddenly her mouth seizes up and she can't seem to say another word. When I ask her if she's going to come and sit at the table she's stuttery, a tumble of cries and whispers, finally she rushes out of the room. I give up, not wanting to press the point. I tell myself it's not the end of the world if her breakfast gets cold, or even if she can't man-age to eat it this once. But I see Bill and Tina look at one another and can tell they think she's rude and putting it on. Well, she *is,* that's the thing, she is and she's not. They've just started slicing the whites of their fried eggs when Nadia bursts back in, grabs the dishcloth from the washing up bowl and plonks it on her head. Then she stands stock still with the water trickling down her cheeks no expression on her face at all, not a wince or blink. She turns at last and goes out of the back door into the garden. It's one of the tragedies of Nadia's life that the more she tries to reach people the more she turns them away from her. Next minute she's back with us, just as Bill is giving his nose a good poke which I'm trying hard not to see. But Nadia, desperate to connect with these cousins, copies him outrageously of course, right down to the quiet removal of the bogey between thumb and forefinger to the strut at the back of his chair. Then she's disappearing out of the back door again with her chicken cushion squashed inside her arm. Slightly batty I know, but I have the sense as she's going out that the chicken is staring right into me with its eye of mirror, its eye of silvered glass. I can't say I'm afraid.

Nadia's such a sight in this bright red dress she'd got in a jumble sale and that she *will* wear though it's at least three sizes too big for her. What with the dress and that dishcloth she's still got plastered to her head, it makes me roar laughing. I roll around in my seat giggling helplessly, the tension of the last few days needing this release. Bill and Tina, I can tell, are not really finding her funny. No doubt they are sorry for her, and sorry for *me* too, though I reckon they won't spend too much pity on me because they'll see me as a fool for putting up with it. *They're both as bad as each other in their own way, Nadia and Tam.* I can hear the cousins saying this to their Manchester friends. No, they'll never see the funny side of it the same way as they'll never really see the sad side either, because these cousins, they're sort of cut off from things, and it's just the way they are.

Later, I cannot find her. I call everywhere when the cousins have gone both in the garden and the house but no reply, then from the bathroom window I catch sight of a bit of red through the branches of some bushes where there was no red before. Staring harder I see that the bushes are shifting slightly although it's a windless day. I go out. When I get close everything goes really still, I suppose Nadia doesn't mean to be found. I stand next to the bush where I thought she'd be but can't exactly see anything, it's all winding twisted branches and clogging leaves. At mid height the bush is a choke of tangles, completely dense, higher up the snaking branches are infiltrated by the blue of sky.

'Nadia?' I say. Then when I look very closely I *do* see her, I see her outline, she's crouched down almost to the ground most of her face obscured by twigs and blackish leaves, I see an eye, she's looking out. 'Bill and Tina are gone now,' I tell her, she'll know that, mind, but what I'm really doing is trying to say I know what she's been going through. Then there's this sound coming from her, a sort of *Uff Uff Uff*, and I know that Nadia's crying, her bottom lip held under by her teeth because she can't let go completely or doesn't want to. I stretch out my hand towards the barrier of scratchy twigs and try to reach her, but Nadia is someone who just won't connect unless *she* wants to. I'm not even sure she's seen me, her eye looks shiny and remote, the expression fixed. She's looking past me, out and up, towards the sky perhaps, or somewhere else; another time or place, a thought, a possibility, a hopeless dream.

Billie-Ricky

Me and my bad Fish feelings. Either I'm this poor fish suffocating in a box, can't breathe, expect to be eaten soon but who knows, or else I'm the victim of some kind of piranha, sharp fish jaws stripping me down to nothing. Here I think of Annette's white pointy teeth, and myself all in bite size chunks. I keep on dreaming of shredded skin, and I'm always imagining the illustration of this pike in the encyclopaedia on the shelf at home. When I think of this drawing though the teeth have gone missing. It alarms me, thinking they'll turn up in my bed or something, spiky and real, and not made out of paper. I'll turn over and they'll jab into me and this horrible Monster Fish will be screeching at me with the voice of Annette, 'I'm gonna get you, Lorraine.' It's so scary having all these thoughts but I really can't help it. My legs have gone weak and shivery just thinking about Annette.

And I know it's because of the net in Annette, those times I keep seeing fish as helpless and floundering, and all caught up. There they are the poor creatures, struggling in the criss-cross of strings never to get anywhere. These fish are, I don't know, whiting, or halibut or cod. They are pale coloured with light blue eyes. Flippy-floppy. Not me this time. They're Sandy. I can't help saying it, but Sandy does bring to mind a fish of this sort when you look at her. It's because her soft mouth opens and closes before words come, and that way her head sways round from side to side as if she's under water all the time. I always have this picture of Sandy swimming towards me, her pale body all wobbles, her eyes the blue of palest glass. Sandy's my cousin, except she's adopted, we're both ten. She's so pudgy looking, and vulnerable sort of, and she'd better watch out because Annette's gonna get her without a doubt. Poor Sandy'll be netted before she knows what's going on and she won't be able to wriggle out of it. I can just see it happening. Annette is Sandy's much older sister, and a stuck up bitch she is, and our two families are all on holiday together in a holiday cottage by this big field next to the river. It'd be brilliant if it weren't for Annette. She's always going on at us two. 'Shut your face our Sandra,' or 'Watch it, Lorraine.' Just when we were going to the weir, Sandy and me, I heard Annette give her a talking to behind this rock. It made my bones go soft. I sat on the other side of the rock, my bones seeming to melt inside me. And I recognised this melting for what it was. Liquid anger. I thought I was going to wet myself at the time.

In the encyclopaedia the pike's lower jaw is extending forward, making the sort of face Annette makes when she's gonna tell you off. She jerks her lip out. It's an ugly sight, this purplish veiny cushion that should be kept well hidden. Her teeth, sharp and pointed are right there though behind the jellified lip, waiting to snap together over anything feeble that can't fend for itself, like Sandy, like me come to think of it, except I'm better at keeping invisible. Anyway she's not my sister, she's got less power over me. She gives me nasty looks that make me have the nightmares about shreds of skin and being stripped to the bone but she can't really do much *to* me. I've seen her shake Sandy twice since we've been here. Shake her and shake her. Child cruelty, it's made my anger run like melted wax.

Sitting the other side of the rock, I'm keeping quiet of course, or Annette will poke her head round, scare me silly. I hear Sandy breathing in a snorey-wheezy kind of way that means she's gone into a panic. 'Breathe through your nose,' Annette's voice squawks at her. Then she says 'That's quite sufficient.'

The bad Fish thoughts come boring into me like hooks. It's the *ffic* in *sufficient*. I picture whole shoals of them come swimming round me, getting tumbled right on top of me in the net. All suffering of course, because of the *suff*. Talk about breathing. Nobody's breathing, not me, not the net-full of fish. And I get a nasty whiff of something, maybe a dead fish has got stuck in one of the criss-crosses, *could* be. It *would* have to be near my nose, wouldn't it. Or maybe Sandy's farted out of fear of Annette, that's more than likely. And now Annette's getting up to go, after more mean talk to Sandy that I've switched off from. 'And make sure you don't go near that weir,' she says as she stomps off across the field in her stupid spiky high heels, her leather skirt creaking as she goes.

The weir is a shelf of dark glass. I love the weir, so does Sandy. We take off our sandals and leave them behind, they're too plain to come somewhere special, it'd spoil the effect. The rush of the water is incredible, it drowns out everything else, it drowns out all thoughts of Annette. It would drown her voice out, even if she were right here and going on we wouldn't hear her. We start walking along the shelf—we always go to the middle of the river and then we crouch down, the cool water rushing over our legs. Oh and we take off our knickers and put them in a pocket, or scrunch 'em up into a ball and keep 'em in our hand if we haven't got a pocket. Then, when we're crouching over the weir like that we both call out at once as loud as we can, 'Billie-Ricky', and we hear the name go into the rushing water noise and it seems as though it will get somewhere, the water will carry it far off, bouncing and echoing, and at last it may even reach the ears of Billy-Ricky, you never know. This is what we'd like. Billy-Ricky is Sandy's real mother. Sandy didn't know her because she was adopted when she was born and she couldn't find out anything about her, except once when she was listening at the door and she heard Annette telling her boyfriend that Sandy was from Billie-Ricky. So that's how she knew and now when we come to the weir we call out her name and we sort of think that she might hear us. When we're staying here we have to share a bed because there aren't enough bedrooms in the holiday cottage for us to have one each. It's good though. At night we make up adventures for Billie-Ricky and tell each other stories in which she has the important part, such as 'Billie-Ricky and the Golden Chalice,' or 'Billie-Ricky and the Sword in the Stone,' or something. The story we like the best is the one where Billie-Ricky is an Amazon warrior who lives in the forest. And it does feel somehow as if this is the true Billie-Ricky. She carries a sword and rides on horseback and goes down the river in a canoe. In this story she had to let Sandy go and be looked after by a normal family because she doesn't live in a house or anything and it wasn't that suitable for a baby, but one day, when Sandy is older, maybe twelve, maybe thirteen, we're not sure, she'll send for her and Sandy will go off and learn how to survive in the wilderness. And so we call now, call out into the whoosh and roar of the weir to remind her that Sandy is here and has a bit of the warrior spirit in her and will easily be able to go over the rapids in a canoe in a year or two. Once I asked my Mum where Sandy came from and she told me Sandy was born in a town in Essex but I don't believe it, it's too boring for somebody as amazing as Billie-Ricky. I never told Sandy, and what's more I never will, it's not worth repeating. And it can't be true, 'cause whatever would an Amazon warrior be doing somewhere ordinary like that? We lean forward together and call as loud as anything, 'Billie-Ricky!' and the weir noise kind of sucks the name up, and sends it on its journey downstream and from there to distant lands. We hope.

What we do next is wee in the water. It feels good letting the wee come out of you and go down the slippery weir mingling with the river. We try and watch to see where our own little pale lemon coloured streamlets will go, but they get lost in the fizz and swoosh and all the foamy flecks collected at the bottom. We know they're there though, twirling and whirling, going along in the flow. It's a great feeling doing this wee here because of the drowning water sound which it's nice to add to with our own little fizzles, the sound we make getting lost in the loud cascade. This place is definitely the best place in the world to have a wee in and this when you come to think about it is more than likely because of the *we* in weir.

WatchTower

Clara says that in one life you can get bound up in *many* lives. She says she'd once got mixed up with two men who behaved as if they thought they were starring in a movie and she herself had almost begun seeing things that way as well. It felt as if everything they did was being performed for the benefit of an audience, even if whoever was watching was quite invisible. Clara wants to talk about how it was with her then. One of the men was her husband, Bill, the other, the best friend of the husband. The three of them were experimenting with friendship. Since, she has become an isolate, but then she was into sharing, by which she meant, being shared. It was flattering, she felt bigger than she felt reduced.

The more so because these men imagined themselves larger than life, saying and believing they were special players with the gift of knowledge about the truth of everything. And they hammered home how things *should* be and railed against the load of crap things tended to be and they were fond of blaming all the shortcomings on the *petit bourgeoisie* and they sat rolling spliffs and scoffing about the *petit bourgeoisie* which they themselves were not, it went without saying, they were not.

There was no friendship or experiment really going on, Clara says and at one level she understood that. Instead there was rivalry which was pleasing. She hadn't realised it to start with but she came to see *she* was the object of both men, she herself. She was the object of desire whereas before she'd been unwanted by anybody. She used to feel plain now suddenly she felt giddily gaudily on top.

On top of the world. On top of the men, her thin breasts, formerly unwanted, jiggling. On top of history; starring in a movie or a play. Yes, she Clara, was also starting to get sucked somehow into the idea that this was the true state of things, and to feel as if they were all in a film or a play together which would be replayed forever. The talking proselytising men would be famous and she too would be famous. She would be a seductress worth remembering.

All the energy led up to one special moment which she promises she'll be coming to by and by. Not yet, because first she wants to give a few details about where they lived then and what life was like. She and Bill had two boys. They were a family living in Basingstoke. The children were not yet in school, the husband was training to be a doctor. He had to give that up eventually though, because he could not overcome the problem of whether he should give water to a dying man, if there was only one cup of water left. If they were all on an island, say. He and the wife and children and Francis the friend, possibly Francis too. So should he?

If a doctor, shouldn't the answer be *yes?* Always and irrevocably *yes.*

But Bill could not decide. It was all extremely difficult, because as well as being a man who thought he knew everything, he was also a man who said he thought he knew nothing. He said the world was full of hypocrisy one way or the other and over the matter of the water he did not appear to know which was the one way and which was the other, did not know the right road to travel. He didn't know if he should care if they all died because there wasn't enough water to go around.

Supposing no rain came, no more rain? Being a small island—Basingstoke, he couldn't travel very far. The road was shorter than it might have been if he'd fetched up somewhere else. But could one choose such a thing, he had the feeling one could not, and didn't this show that after all, one was restricted, there was no such thing as freedom or if there was it was only the freedom to move about inside the confines of a box.

The family lived in a council flat. The husband and the friend sat and deliberated, they rolled their rollies on two fleabag chairs facing the one couch. A couch greasy and spartan. They had found it in a skip and it had always had one cushion missing which was gratifying at the time to the men. Now Clara does not know what they would think, she has not seen either of the men for years. At the time she for one had wished for something better—they said she was *petit bourgeois*, but there you are she was a woman. At least though she believed in the *play*, and believed the three of them had the main parts, and this to them was the most important thing and it redeemed her in their eyes to some extent. Also she had ambition. Her name had started off as Clare but she herself put the *a* in, it was more noisy. She felt like a loud musical instrument. Twang. She had strings and a belly and a mouthpiece. She played the part of a woman. They could all agree what this part meant and that equalled harmony.

But what the men liked best, what both of them really enjoyed was when the Jehovah's Witnesses came on a Saturday. Jehovah's Witnesses trudging slowly up the steep hill of the street, being rejected from door to door but not here. Here of a Saturday afternoon they were most welcome. There was an avid staring out for first sight of them at the bottom of the hill and if they were spotted it was a thing worth celebrating. Bill and Francis opened their beer cans, cheering in a sarcastic way, looking angry but sounding happy. The Jehovah's Witnesses were dots far below, at first indistinct, then just visible as they separated off from shadow. They started to take on form. Dots climbing the hill staunchly turning into individuals who could be seen going into doorways and coming out again. At last they turned into figures passing the window, figures clear and well defined.

The husband and the friend sitting around with a beer—the Jehovah's Witnesses not having any, they were here hoping to save souls, hoping to reclaim this waste for God. Because God saw everything he saw everything that happened in this house. The Jehovah's Witnesses were aware God could not be happy with what he saw. They were doing their level best but the hearts in this house were stony and unreceptive. It made them feel like giving up, but they wouldn't give up. They would try and turn things around if they could.

'But how do you know a rose is beautiful?' asked the husband for the umpteenth time tilting up his lager can, rolling a fag because his performance required it. He'd only just put a rollie out so he added this new one to his little stash for later.

'Just because a rose exists, it doesn't necessarily mean God exists,' said the friend.

The Jehovah's Witnesses had not heard of *contingently*. They were all or nothing types, and they wanted to save souls.

'But how do you know there is a soul?' said the husband and the husband's friend, their voices twining together.

Bill and Francis were sitting in their chairs with a conspiratorial look, a comfortable look. They sat with one leg crossed over the other, they leaned back laconically. The Jehovah's Witnesses sat upright on the couch with the cushion missing. They sat each side of the gap this made.

Clara says because Bill and Francis believed they were starring in a film or in a play they gave a lot of attention to how they did things and how they came across. It wasn't just life to them, it was more real, much more real than that. The two of them sat with their feet up looking a little bored, flicking their cigarette ash in an underplayed but stylised way. They seemed casual but this also was part of the act.

'A soul. Mmm. Where do you think such ideas come from?' asked Francis, his lips salivating on the way to the beer can.

'From God of course, who else?' Is what the Jehovah's Witnesses replied, eyes wide open, round and expectant of disorder. They'd been here before and knew what could feasibly happen. Several Saturday afternoons ago one of the men had pulled a flower out of a vase and torn up the petals and scattered them around the room to prove some sort of a point or other. So the Jehovah's Witnesses steeled themselves when they came in here as they never knew what stupid thing these men might get up to. If they weren't doing God's work they wouldn't dream of entering this place at all. Preaching to the drunks, the drunks with funny words, who were above themselves and looking down. Always looking down their noses. Who knew what to say?

'Just give an example of one perfect thing,' Bill demanded of them.

'A rose,' they said with a cough respectively, one on either side of the gap, wondering about the absent cushion. What happened to it? Did the cushion exist?

'We're just going round in circles,' Francis said to Bill.

'Well you asked them for their opinion,' Clara interjected, jangling a bit, meaning she wasn't satisfied with having such a small part and Bill and Francis had this way of making her feel sometimes as if she was just an extra. 'They've told you their honest opinion, they can't say fairer than that.'

'That's a womanly position, talking about fairness as if that were the issue,' went the men. 'Still it's no bad thing,' they conceded, thinking about the uncomplex socio-politico motivations of the gender. 'But anyway, a rose is just a rose and that's self evident. There's no more to be said. So why does everybody want to put more in than that?'

Bill and Francis themselves, of course, were somewhere else, a different place altogether, on a higher plain where such seedy sentiments wouldn't be allowed to prosper.

'It's just a psychological need,' said Bill to Francis, or the other way round.

Clara at this point in the story was not entirely happy. She wanted a bigger and better part and also she wanted to change some of the script. She says she couldn't help feeling a bit uneasy in the company of the friend and her husband as they sat and watched the window. Bill and Francis could not take their eyes away from the window, so it seemed. They were always watching out for the Jehovah's Witnesses climbing the hill slowly, going into doorways and coming out again quickly. Though more was the pity, not all Saturdays came up with the hoped for goods - sometimes the Jehovah's Witnesses did not appear. This should have pleased the men because it did not please them when they saw the people they were straining to see. But the men were displeased either way. When these people, with their religious quest, came into view the two friends were bursting with angry stares. Francis went pale and flinty, Bill had a sardonic look. But somehow, as Clara said to herself, it was a happy anger, and this was the difference. They saw the religious ones coming up the hill, being rejected from door to door, they were waiting, they were happily angry. Waiting with their answers, gratified if these answers were not understood. They the friends, knew more. The two of them had their wisdom, the Jehovah's Witnesses had not thought things through. Here they came up the hill armed with bibles, steeped in belief. It made the friends shake their heads in mock pity to see this. They popped open their beer cans with angry hands.

Clara wondered, she really wanted to know why it was Bill and Francis were so keen to let the people in. Seeing as how they knew all there was to know about the stupidity and the pathetic nature of belief and they'd already posed all of the questions, and these questions never answered fully, or almost, or even a bit.

'*Why?*' Bill did a fake copy of Clara's questioning voice, making it higher pitched and sillier sounding than it was.

They, heavy with arcane understanding, smiled grimly at the sound of the doorbell. The husband, proprietor of the establishment went to open the door, the friend rustled comfortably into his seat listening to the hallway greetings, then was still.

His name was Francis and this displeased him. He didn't know how his parents could have chosen such a wet name and he couldn't call himself *Frank* that seemed too old fashioned, so he sat on as Francis but trying inside his mind, to deny it was really him. What was in a name anyway, a name was only a label which meant nothing. You just had to be strong enough not to get sucked in, you had to resist your name. A name was neutral, there wasn't any problem, it was just that most people had too much emotion and too much superstition. But he, he Francis, did not and so there was no need to change the name he'd been given. He could un-think it.

His friend, Bill, came back with the visitors into the room which Clara says always felt to her like a film set or a stage. The visitors were cold, they rubbed their hands. They'd been walking up the wintry hill, pressing on door-bells for quite some time now. With no gloves on and why not? They knew it would be cold, did they want to suffer, be seen to be suffering? Was that another point scored in their personal goodness box, another tick in their favour? Brownie points in the eyes of the *Almighty*. Francis smiled a grim smile that was not at heart a smile in the least, Bill smiled back in the same way. Clara moved across to the door, not really wanting to stay for yet another repeat performance of what to her, was a ludicrous puppet show in which Bill and Francis kept on refusing and denying, kept on taunting and being scathing, and the religious side for their part, kept on being religious and talking about roses as proof of God's existence and wanting to turn the world away from wickedness.

'But what *is* wickedness?' said Francis. 'And if God is all powerful where does wickedness come from?' As Clara shut the door and went into the kitchen to do her ironing.

An hour or two went by. Her two boys were at a friend's house but they'd be back soon. It was quiet and cold, the sky outside the window turning rusty pink, a few leaves flying about in the wind. She stopped ironing and stared out. Inside the house the muffle of voices and many patches of silence went on in the way they always did. She knew the rhythms, the breaks and crescendos, and the final conclusion heralded by the massive creaking of chairs. These creaks as the sun went down depressed her. She thought of this wintry Saturday as the emptiness at the end of the world. Slam of the front door and the Jehovah's Witnesses filing past the kitchen window into the street.

The friend came into the kitchen then and leaned across the ironing board and softened and then twinkled his eyes at her. She'd heard him say how he could do this softening and twinkling and it meant nothing, there was no corresponding emotion, only those who saw the effect thought there must be emotion behind it and he was covering up. Anyway they were wrong. She herself didn't know what to think except that she, somehow, had got mixed up in this play or film which was larger than life and was more real whether there was meaning or not. She couldn't say on that point but she felt happier. Her part was increasing. She looked in the mirror later and saw a smiling woman she wasn't used to seeing because usually she did not look in the mirror anyway, but if she did look she saw a sad one or a neutral one at best. She, Clara, was smiling such a lot it was almost an embarrassment. She went to bed smiling and got up that way the next morning. Yes, the smile lasted, she had a warm kind of feeling, and this play or film she was in started to seem far better than the dull life she'd been living. Maybe it didn't matter if there was true meaning there or not.

So Clara moved things to another dimension. He, the friend, liked her, really, he was in love with her and hadn't realised it. She was why he was here all these Saturdays and other days. She intuited all of this in one flash. She'd been aware for some time he'd been smiling at her quite a bit, he'd also stroked her arm more than once. But now suddenly, she saw the truth. She put on redder lipstick and stopped eating the fat from the bacon and salad dressing with garlic in it. She put on eye-shadow. The husband had a sardonic look these days. What he had seen or not seen Clara didn't know. What his feelings were she did not know.

'What *are* feelings?' said Bill and Francis, rolling their rollies, leaning their heads back, spliffs in one hand.

'What are *real* feelings and what are just social constructions?'

The two of them puffing with quiet animation, feet up against the fire fender, she, womanly, bringing in more wood, they, satisfied with the direction their questions were taking.

'Is there anything *other* than social constructions?'

They, leaning back and puffing away, Francis winking at Clara as she went out again.

She saw herself in the mirror in passing. A fast shift of glitter. Was that the mirror or her? She must have been smiling, she could see her lips upturned at each end, she could see her teeth. How did Bill and Francis know what was real and what wasn't? But perhaps they knew more than she did. She was a little humble, she was only twenty four. They were thirty three, perhaps they knew better. She turned back. Francis winked for all to see, meaning Bill. Bill smirking, looking sardonic. She closed the door.

All this energy did lead up finally to the one special moment and this is how Clara puts it: Francis had his charming side which was pleasing, exotic and erotic. He was more and more exciting as the days went on, playing a part that Clara saw as fundamentally *un-Basingstoke*. This appealed. Francis was sunshiny and experimenting with charisma. She was willing to be appealed to on such a point, to be the living proof. She was altogether willing. They lay on the floor awkwardly waiting for something. What they were waiting for was Bill. Francis and Clara lay together, naked from the waist down. Jeans were in a heap to the right side of the door. Bill came in and stood to the left of the door. Ready to begin. They were extra awkward and sometimes they were extra dynamic because of being watched. Clara floated into and out of awareness of Bill, floated into and out of the question of why they were all doing it. She was happy yet not happy with her role. She didn't want it to *be* a role. Francis and Bill said there was nothing else but still she tried to find something more in the eyes of both. She wondered what the word *love* meant. Francis rolled off her when he'd come. She felt cold and immune, untouched. His charisma after all perhaps, was as unreal as he always claimed it was.

Once she'd looked up in the middle of the sex act, as she and Francis squirmed a bit on the floor, as they rolled and wriggled. Bill was right there towering above her, his eyes sharp and observant. Clara had looked up and seen Bill's face and his watching eyes. His eyes frightened her - she saw their emptiness, their intensity, their pain, their fullness, their knowing and unknowing, their despair, their hilarity, their dryness, their lust. His two eyes, all and nothing, just watching her. As she rolled and slid around under Francis on the floor. She saw Bill entirely clearly for just a moment and then his eyes and the rest of him too, began to fade to nothing. It seemed as if the outline of his face and body was just crumbling away, his tall shadow finally becoming softly merged with all of the shadow around them now inside the room.

The Girl Can't Help It

Jessamine has to have it Rick's got this spark in his eye, a special spark, which just when it's made her feel bright, it's made her feel warm and like living again, has turned into something negative with burnout effect. She insists you never know if it was fun or malice that was twinkling there in the first place. You just never know anything much when it comes to understanding Rick, there are so many mixed messages, so much of one kind of thing which could be the very opposite of what you think it is. It's because he's so good in bed that it's worth the time, you wouldn't bother otherwise, not care about what he was up to or he wasn't. But he *makes* you care. And what really gets to her is that *he himself* doesn't really give a damn. When she gets to this point in the dialogue she's building up anger. But she sits on it, swallows it back. 'I really pity his wife,' she says. Beb agrees on that one, but the talk of this special spark she disregards as part of Jessa's dizzy fantasising, an invention to turn herself on and explain the hold Rick has over her. He like the spark is something special.

It's not so much that Beb and Jessa like one another particularly it's that they like the way they see themselves when they're together, that's the thing that counts. They have this *routine* going which they feel good about. Things are different for them now, they've re-invented what they are. Jessamine used to secretly feel plain with her stringy hair and crooked teeth she's never had the energy to see to, she also felt dull and stupid. And this rather flat nose of hers that a boy at school had once joked made her look like a boxer. The words carried on in her mind long after they'd been said, for years this terrible shudder would jolt right through her in the company of men, as if horrifically, she might hear the same thing said again, a nightmare thought that made her unable to look anybody in the eye, that kept her silent. But now, all that's changed, Beb's pointed Jessa in a new direction and she's playing the part of this *dizzy blonde,*—Beb's terminology. And wow, she loves to hear that description of herself, see the admiring look on Beb's face when Beb's talking to other people in front of her. She just starts acting the part, and even at lunch times when Beb isn't around because *he's* there she can slip into it to some extent, like a slinky dress you can zip into in one. Great to have this new self image, before Beb and her *terminology* Jessamine was just a loser. Beb's good at creating something out of nothing, and *believing* in the creation herself, that's what makes her so convincing. Nothing cynical going on, Jessamine can stare into her eyes as much as she wants when she's saying *dizzy blonde* or some equally desirable thing, doesn't matter, Beb can stand it , she's sincere. So Jessa doesn't have to stare now, just to make sure *she's* really the one being talked of, she just accepts it, and that feels good. So she's become what she'd always have liked herself to be. She flings her body around being *dizzy* and it feels naturally her to be doing this, that's the beauty.

'A married man though,' says Beb. She clicks her tongue, but Jessamine's dizzy, and a blonde. It's accepted that she can do things like this, that she can't be any other way. *The girl can't help it.* They giggle together, sigh a bit. Beb's the creative one, the dynamic principle, *femme fatale* of the duo. It's more than a routine going on, there's a burning *need.* What they've done is provided a world together with self identities, new passports to a way of being. They loll forward across their wine glasses as laughter ripples. *He's such a bastard, pity the wife,* comfortable tokens of their fresh currency. Jessamine looks up, sees herself in a long side mirror. Willowy blonde, out on the town, cool as they come. Sort of girl that guys are desperate for. Can't help herself that she's got in with a bad one, it's the way she is. Helpless when it comes to passion.

Beb glances over at the counter where there's a couple of guys, they look back. She yawns. What do they think? She's got a life thank you, she looks past them and away, flicks her eyes down to her watch. No time for em, those guys, she's got a life. *Hard to get* mannerisms she's developed, Beb. Used to be just shy.

Jessamine says there's this certain quality to Rick, this way he has as though he's just about to start dancing. A kind of light grace to him, she doesn't know, she can't quite put it into words but, when she met him, he was doing this sort of *circling,* no, she can't explain. But as if he was just going to dance and he was starting off with swaying to the music, not that there *was* music, that was the thing. No music, no dancing going to happen really, it was just the feeling Rick gave off. And because he has this, because of this funny way of his, he makes you feel that you *also* are going to start dancing, and you'll be dancing together, that's the really exciting thing. What's bad is that there never is going to be any dancing, but by the time you realise this it's already too late for you, you've got pulled in, he has you living in hope and the hope is hopeless. Because it wasn't dancing that really was on the agenda, it was far more likely that kind of body swinging grace of his was just the precursor to taking a punch at you, or someone. It was the way Rick packaged his aggression and that was all it was. But you can see all of this and it can still be too late. He's made you want him to be nice to you, and the worse he gets the more you want that. Jessa's eyes move from sentimental to fatalistic, to sex-aware. *Comes down to that he' s a good fuck.* Beb and Jessa, the laughs that spill out of them, almost to tears. And there are raucous outward-reaching echoes, the guys at the bar glance over.

Beb has been to the country with a man she likes, Robin, they've picked mushrooms in a lane. Robin asked her to carry the mushroom bag. Sweet September. He said to her, 'Take this mushroom.' Robin has a *cultured* voice which she admires and tries to replicate by going lightly with her breath, softening everything, making her speech muffled as though heard through a gauzy curtain, making it slow. It's a strain and an effort being insouciant like this, being classy, but it's Beb's way of trying to sound as he does.

'Oh, thanks,' she breathes, in this snail's-pace way.

Robin is practical, looking for mushrooms at the side of the field, pushing back the taller grasses, searching in the gaps between trees where the soil is mossy and damp. Beb, carrying the mushroom bag, walks just behind. When he finds a mushroom it's all delightful agitation, his body is alert, he jerks forward, dives into the grass, pulls the mushroom out of its hiding place. There's a smell of rank earth as it rips out softly. He hands it over to Beb, tells her to put it in the bag.

At lunchtime, a ruffle of wind and splayed leaves. Could have been romantic and certainly Jessamine was ready for that, her slinky dress mood just coming on, standing there at the door to let the man in. Had to be lunchtime they were together on account of his normal family-man commitments. Couldn't help that. He couldn't have helped it. She, zipping up to expectation, there at the door, watching the leaves swirl. 'Foul day,' he says it is, smell of cigar smoke, of something fermenting, maybe cheese. There in the hall with his *lets get on with it* briskness, his sidling glance. Into the bedroom no fuss. She is stripped of this one simple dress, underneath, nothing. He in his underwear gets down to her.

'You see,' she says later, eyes half crazed for real, because its this or nothing. This, for sex, if she wants to have sex in her life, if she wants it at all. It has to be the short-lived lunchtime experience, it seems it does. There in the room after, with his trousers half done, seems to be dancing, seems. The real thing which lingers is the complexity of smells.

Towards the end of the week here they are in the bar. Jessa and Beb, talking together but eyes straying outwards, straying beyond the two of them as they sit here, being dizzy and fatal, occupying their seats that way. 'I saw Robin,' Beb is saying, they nod and cluck together. Commiseration. Robin's a fool because he can't seem to see what's in front of his eyes, and if only, and then they nod and laugh as though to say he's led a sheltered life, can't help it he is as he is, and Beb's getting her very adult look as though to say she's going to show him, to teach him a lesson good and proper that he'll be unable to forget. Her and her femme fatality, that look to her which says he'll be completely done for, sheltered or not sheltered, is he man or mouse? And Beb has her glittering eye look and *won't put up with crap* face on her that Jessa so admires. The look that tells you Beb's a get up and goer, a winner you wouldn't want to cross. Two guys wink towards them from the counter, indicating, *Would they like a drink, would they like to join them?* Something. But it comes to nothing. Jessa would probably go for it but Beb gets anxious and her hands go all quivery. 'They think we haven't *got* a life or what!' she stage-whispers to her friend. Later the men pass them with smirks, with wry and rude remarks. 'Look at the state of that.' And more, that the women cut off from hearing. Beb freezes them off with a smile meant to chill, to negate. *Who do they think they are.*

Next morning in the High Street Jessamine sees Rick with a woman, hand in hand. *His wife?* Her heart chills and she gets this crumpling feeling, she feels like a piece of paper that has been screwed into a ball, that is light and shrivelled and whatever was written on it is no longer legible. She's in a shop when this happens. Rick and the woman pass by on the outside, hand in hand, arms swinging just a little. *His wife, or somebody else?* Jessamine crumples onto the floor dry as paper. But comes lunchtime and here he is as usual, ringing at the doorbell. He is here with the cigar and cheese smell, nothing has changed. She lets him in red-eyed, he does not notice, or does not appear to notice. 'Foul day,' he says looking out. They stand in the doorway, look at the swirling dampened leaves then Jessa closes the door. He's in a hurry, undoing his jacket while they're still in the hall. But she can't quite manage to be dizzy, she can't quite play the part. 'Whassamatter?' Rick finally says because he has to, because he's seen that pretending not to notice Jessa's mood isn't going to make it go away. He hopes to dispel it with bluntness, with diminishing the importance of whatever has brought it on. 'Cheer up,' he says. 'May never happen.' But the cheap-cheesy way of him, the words, bring on a bout of despondency and next minute Jessa's in tears, Rick with his hand half way to her crotch at the time. *Ah Christ he doesn't have time for this.* They stand awkwardly together not quite into the bedroom and then Rick says, 'Well if you're gonna be in this sort of mood I might as well be off.' And then she's afraid of losing him, afraid he'll really go. He'll be gone, there'll be no-one. She'll be like Beb then, with nobody. This thought on top of the sight of the swinging held hands which she can't get out of her mind. Makes her sob the more, her eye makeup starts to run. 'Oh Jesus Christ,' he says and turns towards the door. Then she's after him, pulling at the nearly re done jacket, grasping at one of the sleeves, leaping up at him. A wild thing, she's a wild thing.

'Who was that woman?' she shouts dramatically, her voice nearly hoarse from the strain of it.

'Oh I see,' he says swinging back to face her. 'So that's it.' He's ready to be flattered by the sight of her jealousy, pacified by it, made tender. Could even be an interesting prelude to sex, Jessa jealous like this. But something in him turns when he looks at her, he sees her as a desperate character, sad as they come, up till now he's thought of her with some kind of awe, a mystery woman beyond the sphere of the domestic that he never has to feel guilty about. She screams up and into his face, a wash of snot suddenly gushing down over her lips. He feels pity which comes out as hatred, and no trace of understanding. He strides forward, gets the door open, meaning to be off, but she's right there on the step next to him, fast as he is, just as intent.

'No,' she's crying out. He sees her mouth with strands of saliva in a tremor from the force, sees her eyes squeezed right up. What he does is go for her between the eyes. Between the eyes, that's where his fist goes and then she's down on the floor of the hallway and he's really gone. Jessa struggles back into the flat, crying in fits, first thing she does is call Beb. Beb comes round. Beb sees Jessa through the clear but dull glass of the door panel, face swollen from crying, eyes already blackening from the blow. She's a mess, broken reed of a figure. Shock to see her. Looks as if she's been in the ring, been in a fight, has come off the loser too stupid to concede before it came to this. No sign of *dizzy*, very far from it. And though it's all silent out there on the doorstep Beb can tell that Jessa's open mouth is letting out a scream, when the door opens she'll drown her out with sound. Beb would like to walk away, she can't really handle the sight of Jessamine as a loser, a mess of gore and grief. Beb, her eyes hardening. Can't bear what she's seeing but it's too late to turn, the door's already opening.

A comfortable morning, some sunshine, no rain, sting of autumn, moisture of the dew. Mushrooms in the lane. Robin the hunter-gatherer foraging in the field grass, Beb with the mushroom bag following on. 'Here's one,' he says, handing over a fine creamy coated mushroom which he's just torn neatly out of the earth. Certain and clear cut, Beb feels a surge of good feeling. She takes the mushroom into her hand busily, drops it into the mushroom bag.

'Here's another.'

Beb has her arm held out fairly straight like a signpost, her hand is flat and still, palm upwards. The deposited mushroom is a maggoty messy thing, all frayed. It sits on her open hand the stalk a froth of writhing. Worms. The end of the stalk is hidden as the worms rise upwards, ever higher. Beb standing trancelike, her hand and arm in this fixed position as though all decision making ability has been zapped from her. A kind of numb acquiescence. She sees the dark corrugated base of the mushroom and the whitish wriggling movement of the rest of it but her eyes are mystified if anything. Like a child for whom a new experience has not yet been defined so they don't know how to see it. Is it good, or bad, or something else again? As though she's awaiting instructions on how to feel, her arm, a signpost without direction. Robin is away in the grasses, avid, occupied with the task of looking. Beb stands still in the lane her hand held out in supplication, humble, as though maybe she doesn't expect to find a blueprint after all.

Rick is back in Jessamine's life, they've made up. She sits in the bar with Beb, a Friday night. Feeling needed, feeling that life isn't passing her by, she's right in there. She nods her head at Beb about her lover, unearthing observations. 'That smile of his,' she's saying. 'It can draw you right in, you know.' She gives a dizzy giggle, wouldn't be wanting to be Beb at any cost for all her strength and independence. Because, because, it's true to say Beb hasn't got anybody, has she. *She* Jessamine, would much rather be just what she is, a dizzy blonde. 'Oh but though, a married man,' Beb says, playing her part. The two women sigh together, two men over at the bar look across.

'That smile of Rick's, ya know, hard to tell if there's any humour there in it at all. Definitely over the border into vicious. Sinister, or what. But, well it's hard to put into words, I mean to say there's still that something that makes you disbelieve what you're seeing and even though you've got your eyes open he makes you, you know, doubt your own powers of observation. Maybe his smile is o'kay, maybe its just warm. But no, no forget all that anyway.' Jessa waves her arm, animated by this new inspiration she's getting. 'What it is is, Rick's like a pendulum. He has this way about him. He'll swing one way and then he'll swing the other. One minute he'll be in ice cold territory.' They squeal-laugh at Jessa's description causing a bit of interest over in the bar region, not that they care. 'All at once though he'll swing right back into warmth zone, and it'll be as if he'd never left it and you'll already be forgetting you'd ever seen him being different.'

TailBacks

Lemon dog on the road, dog we cannot see. Dying dog spread sedentary at the top of the low Norfolk hill. All *we* see is the long line of cars, the dazzle red of lights against November grey. Afterwards, what hurt me most was that I'd been unable to see what was happening just one hilltop away from my moment of bliss.

My name is Jan. On this day, the 6th November, a Saturday at three-thirty in the afternoon, I sit impatiently in the passenger seat of an unfamiliar car with Matthew, a man I barely know, beginning to be afraid we won't make it to Laura's wedding service. We're both friends of Laura, living in nearby villages, hence the idea of sharing transport. Strange really, that Laura who's day it was, doesn't come into the story. I'm getting tense. I keep on looking at my watch.

Line of red tail lights up the hill, reflecting on the road and on the shiny white fence posts which jut out here and there in the scraggy hedge to our left. Beyond this hedge a flat brown field, already darkening. An unpromising setting for the sudden flare of passion. On closer inspection the field turns out to have one unruly dip somewhere towards its centre where two ragged thorn bushes stand out against the sky. None of this can be seen from the car though with its windows closed against the cold and the low lying mist. Fields of vision are so curtailed.

'Oh no,' I blurt out, looking desperately at the time. 'We're just not going to make it.'

Low keening sound of the dying dog sat spread with folded paws. Smooth yellow Labrador at the centre of a river of red. This dog seeming strangely half-lion, half-human, with its head held high, eyes part-total confusion, part-knowing. Sharing its mixed emotions with the small crowd of people at the summit of the hill. Sense of being stunned, yet also, there's this recognition of death. The life passing out of that yellow body so slowly, it's almost serene. And that terrible keening full of pain and fear, seeming to cry out for all of us who can hear it.

But in Ashwicken I did find bliss, precious lost to the world seconds which I am now unable to imagine. That mad moment, the blind cut off quality of it which excited me then, while it lasted. I think I deeply believed in that intense and isolated act, and anyway it's not the job of passion to be wise, to understand the wider context, to feel such a morbid thing as shame. It is what it is, a pure thing. Perhaps it's the loss of this purity which is the tragedy here, and the letting in of everything, of all the pain surrounding that one bit of starlight. In the brown earth field beyond the scraggle-hedge we didn't know about the dog although it was so close to where we lay, so very close, just a tail of lights away.

'It's got to be an accident, hasn't it. Can't see a thing though, nothing at all.' For there's no movement out on the hill, and behind us now cars are lined up right back to the corner. All static.

'I think we should toast the bride.'

We climb out of the car with two found picnic cups and a bottle of Orangina, stand on the bumpy verge, just stand there, quietly, emptily, as though mentally freeing ourselves for the start of a journey. 'Let's go into that field,' one of us says. 'A walk.' For nothing's going to be happening here, it's obvious.

We hold down the barbed wire within the hedge and step across, one after the other. As I twist and turn through I look up the line of tail lights to the summit of the hill, catching a quick sight of lemon. Or perhaps not, perhaps this is what I imagine later after I have seen the dying dog.

And here we are in a small dip of the earth field where a few sprouts of stiff grass give a relative sense of comfort, and in complete seriousness open the bottle and share the fizzy orange equally, pouring it with precision into the two held out cups, a ritual to mark a triumphant arrival in an unknown territory. 'To Laura,' we both say. 'Laura and Richard.' And then we look at one another.

What I see is a man I've never really noticed before, as a man, as a sexual being I mean. He has fairly close knit eyes and a mouth held tight by habit, which looks as though it could release wonderfully into a softer, looser form. I take the three steps necessary to reach him, wanting to touch that mouth and kiss it, and then I hesitate. *How does he see me?*

We've walked a short way into the field in the shallow valley of that one small dip. The grasses are taller here, then there are the little thorn bushes which make me happy to see them, as though they are an emblem of the two of us, a welcome party for our need. We sink down between them where the grass is tallest. I see the line of cars on the far side of the hedge all quite still. Then I see the arms of this man, this exciting and desirable stranger. I see the hands, hairs at the cuff edge, those slightly furrowed eyes speaking of secrets which melt out now in my look, and his lips, the mellowing shift of them which makes me wince with pleasure or pain. At moments as vivid as this it's sometimes hard to know which, but maybe it's a blend of both, or maybe finally they are the same.

All the time we fling and fumble and set upon one another deliciously in the cold afternoon we have forgotten to feel, the same dying is going on up the road only closer now to its finality, the keening probably louder, the eyes of the onlookers more impotent, more grieving. As I stretch my whole body in an unbelievable surge of strength and then hold still, torturously waiting, feel the orgasm moving through every part of me releasing me into bliss, that dying is going on slowly without cessation, moving with no hesitation in that one so certain direction. Later it comes as a shock to me, realising that my passion and this dying were happening together, as if they were linked these two events.

The cry of the dog has lodged itself inside me, forced my breath away. Sitting in the car I grasped at my throat I remember, trying to alleviate the ache, trying to push off this sense I had of being strangled. I coughed and spluttered needing to find air. And I knew then that a very significant part of me would always remain stuck on that hill, that I'd never be entirely free of it. A million half formed questions rise up in me, and the answers are always equally unsatisfactory. The dog has brought me to a wider awareness, for better or worse.

Lying in the dent of earth we have created with our own joint bodyweight. Grass stems flatten beneath us, crisp and feathery grass heads fanning round our faces in tune with our pumping movement and the slow exhale of our breath. My body, fluttering down to calm, lying in its pool of wet, the wet turning cold against a bare section of my buttock, bringing me to.

'Jan.' Matthew is pulling himself up, zipping his trousers, smoothing his hair with the other hand.
    'Yes,' I finally say.
    'That was so amazing.'
    'And for me.'
    We start to eye lock. It's incredible how quickly you can weld yourself into someone. I draw my eyes away. 'What about the cars?' I haven't looked, somehow I can't rouse myself to.

'Still not moving,' Matthew tells me, and I am slightly unnerved, just for a second at the way he's more able to deal with the outside world than I am at this moment. He's seen my sudden frown, we both laugh.

I'm brushing the remains of grass heads from my skirt. Velvet, sadly, it doesn't look too good I have to say. Matthew raises his eyebrows to make me smile. I smile. 'But look,' I tell him. 'The cars!' At the top of the small hill they've started up. You can see the wink of lights, slow but definite movement. We start to run fast across the stretch of earth. Racing back to the car there's a lightness to us, a buoyancy, this great free feeling. Don't know what happened to the cups and the orange bottle, I suppose we left them behind with the thorn trees.

Now we're in the car, not talking but hand squeezing and enjoying the silence. And very slowly we are driving forward. 'What's that?' I blurt out suddenly. My voice is afraid, I can hear the shake in it. Then we see the dog and winding down the windows, out of sympathy, in a desire to connect in some way, we hear the terrible moaning noise issuing from the just-open mouth. The lemon fur is heavily red where it rests against the ground. Looking down I see that the animal is sitting in a thick and darkening pool. Those eyes! Staring and blinking, staring and blinking, the dog sedate as a sphinx, asking you questions which you cannot answer. Seeming to preside over the hill and over everything in this sunless landscape like a fabled monster of classical antiquity. Our car, going slowly like the ones before us, arcs out into a wide curve in homage, the way they all have done. And I'm ice-cold numb.

Matthew, could have been he swallowed the experience and it passed through his system leaving no trace. Or maybe it entered his life, became an obstruction strangling the illusion of happiness, leaving tailbacks in the heart. I see him now and then and we even speak, now that some time has passed. But we were never like that again together. We didn't make it to the wedding reception, neither of us feeling equal to the demands of party-ing, couldn't bear to think of it. What we did was drive back by the King's Lynn road on the other side of the hill, not wanting, of course not wanting, to pass the dog again or even see the empty space of road where it had once been.

The Sadness Story

Celine has this open way with her. Such a direct eye she has, and a clear gaze which reassures. She's so unaffected and simple, you feel at once that at last you've met somebody *real*. Someone who sees things as they are and is telling you that without dolling up or doing down. And she doesn't just agree with everything said to her. She seems to balance things, weigh the words, to see if they fit the truth as she's observed it. You can see her thinking seriously about what people say to her, trying the ideas out for sense. I suppose most of all, it's the candid smile that gives Celine such an air of sincerity. One extra thing, her body language. Celine is one of the least posing people you could hope to meet. She comes across as totally natural. The only thing it's not so easy to see is why Celine is telling this story, I mean, she hardly knows us. But I suppose that's just part of the way she is.

Celine is an actress. What she tells us is there's this *perfectly lovely man*, desperately in love with her. But she doesn't say these words in the sort of affected or silly way words like this are often said. She's just speaking matter of factly, with a sprinkling of the wistful. The words used are appropriate for the story, that is all. You couldn't have said she got any pleasure from what she was saying, or the thought behind the words. 'There is this perfectly lovely man,' she says. 'A leading actor with the Royal Shakespeare Company. He sent me the most exquisite, the most gorgeous, bunch of flowers for my first night.' Celine spreads her arms very wide to try and give a fair impression of the fullness of that bouquet. 'Beautiful roses. They must have cost a fortune.'

She shakes her head sadly and lifts up her hair from the underside, strand after strand, and lets it run through her fingers. Nothing contrived about this, though in the abstract it might sound that way. No, all perfectly natural. She shakes her head, even sadder. 'It's crazy,' she says. 'There's this perfectly nice man. I really like him but . . .' Here Celine looks troubled. 'I just can't feel anything for him. I just can't. It isn't there.' She presses her hand to the front of her body, squeezing in her left breast. 'So. Well, what can you do? And sexually, he didn't really do anything for me either. There was nothing.' Her hand slips down, as though to darkness. 'And, and, he keeps phoning me up all the time. He's just crazy about me.' Her voice is building up now as though to reach sky. The sky I picture is overcast, clouds are about to burst, it will rain tears. 'He really does love me—such a lot.'

Celine pulls her hair up from the nape of her neck section by section, holds it all together, passing it from hand to hand. Then, when she's got all those loose bits worked into one bunch she takes an elastic band from her pocket and puts the hair into it, out of sight. A tail of hair which she swings now from one shoulder to the other. 'Whenever I get back to Town he just phones me all the time. All the time.' Her voice is fairly casual, mild and unhurried. Nothing flustered about her delivery, and you've never received the feeling she's desperate to tell you these things. What it seems like most of all is thinking out loud. It hardly feels as if you yourself are necessary to the process, but on the other hand you do have this sense of being included somehow, of being important. You listen intently, you want to, out of some kind of empathy she makes you feel. It's the very opposite of audience factor, I'm sure of that. You are here incidentally, don't forget. She didn't plan for this to happen and she doesn't need you to hear her. But well, you're here aren't you, and she being really open has nothing to hide, and it's not as if she minds telling you. So you feel flattered in a strange kind of way, and make sure to listen with interest so as not to put her off. And it's true you feel involved with what Celine is saying, you really feel involved.

'He asked me, *What did you do today? And so I told him. This and that. I went swimming. Just getting ready to go away. You know I'm going away tomorrow. Packing and that mainly. And then in the afternoon Alan came round. We talked and had a cup of coffee. I had to get ready to go away. I'm packed now. In the evening I watched a film.* And he said, *Fine.* And we said goodbye and that was that and then, half an hour later he phoned back again and he said, *What do you do that for? What did you say that for?* And I said to him, *What do you mean?* Because I wanted him to come out and say what was the matter with him. He never comes right out and says what's the matter, and I wanted him to say it. And he said, *You know. What you said to me.* So I said to him, *About Alan, you mean? That Alan came round?* And he told me, *Yes.* Well, he knows about Alan, he knows I still see Alan sometimes. But he's so jealous you see. So he said to me, *When you get back* - that was in two weeks—*phone me.* And I said to him, *No.* And he said, *What do you mean, No? Please phone me Celine. Please phone me when you get back.* And I said, *I'll phone you if I want to speak to you, not because you tell me to.* And then she says she said to him, *Trust me.'*

Now Celine is easing some strands of her hair out of the elastic band and twisting them forward over her ears. And she's pulling more of the hair out and spreading it. More and more strands of hair, her fingers working fast. Her eyes look dim now she's not speaking, as though she's taking a break and isn't fully here at the moment. And she fizzles the fine hair in her fingers and fans it out. She holds the spread out hair for a minute then takes her hand away quickly. The ends of her hair fall abruptly down onto her cheek and she scoops them up again quite deftly and holds them in the spread fan. And all the time she's extracting more and more strands from the tail at the back of her head till there's hair in her neck as well as at the sides of her face. Her hair's all mussed up, sticking out at every kind of angle.

Then suddenly she says, 'And then I came back. And I was very tired, I'd been touring. I only just phoned one or two people and then I crashed. I was so tired I just had to sleep, didn't want to speak to anybody just then, you know.' Celine goes silent and then at last makes this face of regret, which tells you we are now at the crux, coming up to the punch line. She shrugs her shoulders as though to say, *Life's sad, but what can I do?* Her lips have taken on this puckered look. And we know it's the sadness of things, the sadness which Celine sees, making the puckering happen.

'So, I didn't phone him. There were lots of messages from him on the answerphone. Hundreds of messages left for me. Well, that's it.' Celine's voice trails away, her eyes are quiet and gentle. Nothing more to tell you, almost. 'I'm not ready for that kind of relationship. I don't want to get involved like that with anybody at the moment. I'm just unable to cope with it. He's a perfectly nice, perfectly lovely man. It's just me, you see, and he doesn't understand where I'm coming from. I mean he can't just be a friend, or as a lover he can't just be casual. He doesn't see things that way, he wants what he wants. And I'm not ready for that. I can't handle that sort of thing.' Celine makes a face which has an angelic quality to it, eyes uplifted and held still. She keeps them fixed for a moment in that slightly raised position. 'I wouldn't want to get involved in that way.' Her voice is softly quiet, what you could call a tender whisper. 'The next day, I phoned him and he was out. I phoned him again and left a message but he hasn't rung back. He hasn't returned the call.'

Celine shakes her head at us with infinite sadness as though there are fates at work beyond her personal control. Fates, fate. Her sad destiny. The sad destiny of this *perfectly lovely man*. Sadness of meetings which do not happen because of fate, the idea of always just missing. Never-quite-touching sadnesses, always-fading-away sadnesses, the huge sadness of the irrevocable and unstoppable.

Her hair is all pulled out of the band now, it swings loosely round her face to the shoulder, slightly fluffed out because it had been tied up like that. Celine starts to flatten it down with her hand and to shake it back, away from her face. 'He never returned the call. Well.' The well-it-can't be-helped sadness and we,-none-of-us,-can-help-what-we-feel-even-though-we-might-be-fools sadness, of her smile.

Astral Bodies

'It's because of the Lisbon Earthquake I have this acute fear of buildings and of being trapped inside them. It's the reason I keep picturing walls crumbling and turning to rubble all around me. It's the reason I can never eat an orange. Have I never told you this?' says Sharon to her sister Isabel over the phone one early afternoon in late February when the wind is cold. And yes, it's one of the things Sharon is always telling her, though it wouldn't be Isabel's way to point this out. Isabel is busy brushing her hair by the mirror in the hallway, getting together her gloves, her shopping trolley, preparing to go out. It's certainly on the chilly side. She shivers.

Frank, Isabel's husband is asleep by the radiator in the room at the front of the house, with the TV on, or the radio. Isabel can hear the faint background droning from where she's standing. She's feeling in her pocket for her keys. '1755. November the First. I can picture that day so clearly. It was the day I was to enter the Convent of Santa Maria. I see myself as I was then, fresh faced, dark hair tied up in a knot, that plain grey dress I wore. I remember standing in this large bare room, looking out through a little door which led to the inner courtyard when I felt this curious shaking all around me. A rumbling, yes a deep heavy rumbling. Under my feet and everywhere. I was fascinated before I was frightened. That was my first sensation.' Sharon says this is what happened in one of her previous lives.

Neither Sharon nor Isabel were so bound up in the every-day as they might have been, neither of them caring for what *was,* half as much as what was not. There was something about the present moment which was too troubling, too perilous for their taste. Both sisters preferred to dwell on other possibilities, they liked the idea of being able to get to somewhere else. It was her past lives that Sharon cared about whereas Isabel liked to predict what the future had in store. The comfort of the past, the promise of the future. In this way they complemented one another.

The most troubling thing was seeing how happiness could be whisked away, leaving you bereft. It was beyond your control, you were powerless. It always seemed to Isabel as if there was only this fixed amount of power to go round. One minute it was there with you, then the next you'd lost it altogether. Both sisters were deeply affected by this idea. Sometimes it felt as if the two of them were rivals for the little bit of power available. Maybe sisters usually saw things that way. When they had the power they gloried but when it went away again they felt robbed, suffering an acute sense of loss, also resentment. To start with each sister secretly blamed the other, then they came to see it was life itself, life which imposed its limitations on your desires. The destruction of happiness was what made them conscious of the past and future. It made them think, it was also what maimed them. They looked around for escape routes from the losses they couldn't bear to contemplate. How to remain optimistic in an impossible world, how to keep on believing there was always going to be another chance? Surely they could find a way.

People called them the Bellamy sisters as if they were a double act. As though they could be about to break into a duet at any minute. And there was a time when they both did the kind of smiles that would have gone with this, audience-aware, heads thrown back as though for a photo.

Sharon was a year younger but still she was slightly bigger. The two sisters did look very alike though nobody ever thought of them as twins. Sometimes, Isabel recalls, they pretended they *were* twins, being glad when they were given the same clothes, but nobody was taken in. The reality was, they were complementary opposites, and she thinks they both may have realised this by instinct, but nobody else perceived it, even so. That the two sisters were unbelievably different was all people ever seemed to see. Sharon was the golden girl. At school her exercise book pages were dotted with gold stars because she'd answered all the questions fluently, writing her sentences in bold round letters. Isabel could only manage blots and jumbled squiggly forms and couldn't think of what to say. Sharon held a buttercup under the chin of Isabel to test the quality of her inner light. She held her sister's head sideways, looked doubtful, Isabel shrinking in full bitter knowledge of her fundamental dullness.

Then Isabel discovered numbers. She had an aptitude, could imagine all those separate little entities splitting and increasing to infinity. She saw them in her mind, coursing through empty space and she had the instinctive drive to go with them as if she was flying into the future. Sharon found it hard to multiply and divide, even seeing the signs for these functions gave her a deep depressed feeling. The idea of algebra was something she didn't even want to think about. Isabel soared on to her new heights. Sharon started reading history books.

The two of them went ice-skating. Isabel thinks of them in those identical heliotrope dresses made by their grandmother. She remembers the dresses with mixed feelings. Funky velvet with two-tone beeswing undersides. Sharon filled her dress nicely, Isabel was skinny as a bean-stick, with knobbly knees. The dress, gorgeous in itself, hung on her body, all flopsy and wasted. She was shorter so it came lower down her leg making her feel like a frump. Isabel was ungainly, she wobbled violently on the ice and then fell. Bruised purple fruit. Whereas Sharon could leave the bar easily and glide with grace almost from the start, Isabel even dreaded lacing up her skating boots. Once the skates were on and you were hobbling across the coarse matting to the rink it felt as if there was no going back, you were practically a lost soul. Sharon exulted in her golden aura, Isabel felt sickly pale against the heliotrope velvet. It drained all the colour out of her eyes leaving them like puddled rainwater. 'Never mind,' said Sharon, smoothing the nap of her dress preparatory to skating away. But surprisingly, Isabel found her feet able to do the ice dances. She could memorise the sequences and repetitions and then reproduce these endlessly in careful slightly wooden steps. Sharon had the natural grace but she couldn't quite master the necessary routines. How could Isabel, or anyone, be able to do that? Sharon was envious. When she was eighteen she turned her back on the whole process and found a boyfriend.

'Joe, d'you remember him? My first,' she'd sometimes say to Isabel, even now, thirty two years later. 'We'd definitely met each other in a past life but not too happily. It was in the autumn of 1642, as a matter of fact, just before the Battle of Edgehill. We were both serving under Essex. I remembered Joe clearly the minute I saw him again. Things weren't destined to work out this time around either, but maybe we'll get together properly in another life. You never know.'

Sharon saw her past lives very clearly. She never saw her future ones or had much idea of how they were going to be. The past was what absorbed all Sharon's enthusiasm and her eyes would light up when she said things to Isabel like, 'It's as real to me as you sitting there now across that table,' or 'it's just as if it had happened only yesterday.' And then she'd go into very specific detail and all the ins and outs of where exactly she was in that past life moment she was talking about.

'I was strolling through the orange grove which belonged to the Convent. A late harvesting was taking place. Somebody leaned forward and passed me a segment of the fruit. I can see my hand stretching out to receive it, the sun glinting across my spread open fingers. Flecks of bright yellow and gold. Vivid.'

Isabel sometimes used to ask Sharon how she knew she wasn't just imagining it. 'Oh no,' Sharon would go with this secret smile she'd developed, her eyes completely focussed on something else, something invisible to Isabel. 'Imagination doesn't come into it. I can see everything very clearly. It really did happen that way. I was there in that other life. It was me, despite appearances.' Then she might look thoughtful for a minute and say, 'It wasn't my last life though, it was the one before that.' Sharon would tell Isabel all this patiently as though she was talking to someone with limited understanding. Mainly Isabel just nodded. What else could she have done? It was a simple fact that neither sister could really communicate with the other. They lived in separate worlds.

Isabel liked to try and picture what might happen in the future, wanting to be in the know. She dreaded the idea of being somebody bewildered by new circumstances, stranded in some past backwater that no-body cared about. She was anxious to be at the forefront of whatever tomorrow might bring, and she was always looking out for signs of what was coming, liking the idea of having some sort of insight and the ability to predict correctly. Isabel enjoyed acting on hunches. Sometimes it felt as if the future wasn't written down in advance but might be open to persuasion. Her most cherished and private thought of all was the hope that she could influence what was to happen and be able to turn things in her favour. Seeing if she could was the secret inner excitement of her life. That, to Isabel, was winning in no uncertain terms. Hidden within the outer drabness of her everyday appearance was this shining spark of possibility. It felt as if she could ride the spark out of the body she inhabited and take herself to another place altogether. She could ride inside it to a future world. This was as golden a thought as anything Sharon herself had ever come up with.

'All Saints Day, 1755. It's hard to believe it's over two hundred years ago. I can see myself standing there quietly in that vast room as if it was another person, but it *was* me. I can remember the thought I was having as the room rumbled and first one crack and then another, appeared in the streaked marble floor. It was the day I died, of course.'

Isabel feels as though she ought to say she's sorry to hear that, or something equally sympathetic. She can't quite bring herself to do it though. Not only that, she's got one eye on the clock through all of this and is conscious the time's getting on. 'What were you thinking of?' she asks at last, knowing she has to make some response. Then she's buttoning herself into her grey woolly coat, taking down her plaid scarf, folding it over her front cross-wise, putting on her habitual going-out face in front of the mirror. Half a lipstick smile though a little absent. Half a frown.

'The taste of oranges,' says Sharon. 'I must've told you.'

Suddenly the door's opening and here's Frank yawning in the hallway. 'Bit cold out there Love,' he says to Isabel. 'You don't really need to go shopping today, do you? I mean, you went yesterday, and, the day before that. The forecast says it could even snow.'

'No, I have to,' Isabel says quickly, wheeling forward her shopping trolley. There are things I have to get. I don't mind the weather.'

Going down the High Street, going over to the other side of Town. Going fast to keep the cold at bay. She's still on the thin side though not as stick-like as she used to be. Going fast, liking the walk, not bothering to wait for the bus. She's wondering what today might bring.

When she gets to the Amusements she goes in. At once she feels the anxieties of life slipping away, she feels light and buoyant, as though flying would be possible. Flying far from everything dismal, flying to somewhere new. And she's calling 'Hello,' to one or two of the other regulars. She's been coming here for some time now after all, she knows everybody present. It's a world kept to itself though. No-one who comes here forms any kind of attachment in the world of the everyday. If they pass one another on the street they probably don't notice it. They wouldn't want to. This is a special sealed-off place.

Isabel jingles the money in her purse as she walks down the first aisle of fruit machines. Will she win, won't she? Time to begin.

In one moment she's losing heavily, she's as down as at any time she can remember. It gives her pain. It means her predictions aren't what they should be, she's rubbish, she's lost her luck. It gets to her, she slumps her shoulders down. But still, nothing's ever final in the Amusement Hall, there's always tomorrow waiting and she'll be a winner in the end. Anyhow, she can't give up. Can't and won't. She just can't stop. And then sure enough, there's a turn-around, just as she knew there would be. All at once she's right on top of things, she's surging forward, going ever higher. She's making it, hitting all the jackpots, she's a winner who can't do anything wrong. It's ecstasy. The money's pouring out at her from this fruit machine, that fruit machine. In triumph Isabel works her way round the *One Armed Bandits*. And at the same time another, quiet excitement is building up. Because she's getting closer to the main thing here, getting closer to the horses, the horses that form the pinnacle of the Amusement Hall, as far as Isabel's concerned. The horses are the real reason she's in this place. For the horses, she doesn't know why it is, have the power to take her out of herself. But why stop to question it? All she knows is she can lose herself in this completely other world. Can fly into it, be part of it, and leave her troubles far behind, yet at the same time, her real everyday world will not be turned upside down or misplaced. She can get back to it the minute she leaves this space. It will still be there. The power of the horses will not intrude beyond her wish. Isabel puts her faith in the horses for that, knows they won't let her down.

And so at last she moves over to the joy of her life, the *Magic Gee-Gees,* six lanes of plastic horses set out in their oblong case, each horse in its marked-off strip of green. Each horse with its own special number and colour. Which one will she be today? *Place Your Bets.*

The lights flash and she puts her money in the slot. She's going for the Green. It's Number One. She knows it's a winner. She knows, she knows.

And the horses jerk raggedly forward, White's spurting ahead quickly, Pink is running along second, Yellow hasn't left the starting line, Blue and Red are already in a tangle to the side. But Green, Green is steady, Green is moving forward. A few setbacks when Isabel's heart is agitated, but no, no need to worry. She's seeing it all very clearly. Look, Green's past Pink now,

Green's coming up to White. And White's stumbling, White's about to fall. She raises her hands to her mouth, a small shriek rises up. Green's coming up to the finish and then, oh no, she can't believe this, because she wills and wills that this isn't about to happen. It's Blue, Blue's suddenly there and past the post and the race is over. Ah well, she was very nearly right, she rationalises. It's a matter of concentrating harder, that's all. She can be a winner, she can really get there, the horses will take her to where she wants to be.

No sooner has one race finished than the whole thing starts up again. No gaps. All the lights are flashing, bright with promise. She selects the right-sized coin.

Isabel's got a feeling for Red this time. Number Four. She's got such a strong feeling it's as if she herself *is* Red, she's moved all her being to the inside of the red plastic horse. She sees her normal self in the drab winter coat standing by the *Magic Gee-Gees,* her shopping bag resting by the foot of the case. Sees herself for a minute like a stranger, as if that pale and angular woman there isn't herself any more. Her real self is here in the horse. The lucky winner. She feels altogether different from how she'd felt only a moment ago. The woman in the grey coat is watching from outside the glass.

Then comes the mechanical voice, coaxing, commanding, bringing the future to life. 'Place your bets *naowwww* for the next race.'

Lady of the Spin

End-of-season gloom on the sea-front. Early afternoon in September and the world's gone semi-dark. Ms Della Gira sitting in the 'FishWorld Nautical Gift Shop', is pensive and yet restless. At last she rises from her seat, glides over netting, boxes of fishmeal, buckets-and-spades, her far-off eyes gazing *Where the lilies blow,* in this *Space of flowers,* this *silent isle.* And climbs the mounds of rope and rubble. A silver chalice, a bejewelled hand. Serene white hand, at which Brenda stares.

Container of whitish powder. A silver bowl. Ready to begin her life's task! Ms Della Gira presses a hidden button, the bowl starts to revolve. She tips in the powder which quickly turns sticky, raspberry red. Then takes up a wooden wand, begins to spin a magic web.Twirl of the tub, streaks of silver and red. Ms Della Gira holding wistful eyes low, bending her lithe body to the rhythm of the spinning. What does she wish for?

Brenda, tall on a stately horse which shifts in a little circle as rain patters against the window. Patters and batters in the grey and silver light. *As she rides down, as she rides down.* And the spinner twists and weaves.

Ethereal face of the spinner, her quivering eyebrows, pale-rose lips. The mystery of Ms Della Gira and the melancholic charm of this strange emporium where she spins and spins her life away. Brenda, cantering across the gritty floor, hears her name whispered on the wind. '*Sir Lancelot.*'

'Yes,' she calls back, riding boldly across the greensward and the long romantic road which twists and turns. A river down below, high hills on either side. A plume, a shield, a red-cross knight. Her bells ring out.

Whirring of silver and red, the white hand with tapered fingers, the wand gathering up fine spun thread. Gritted surface of the floor, a real and every-day roughness which Brenda's pained by seeing. But a rush of wind through the misty window restores her, the sky outside is purple now. Looking out, Brenda thinks, 'There's going to be a storm.' The sea looks angry, jets of foam shoot up, cascade over the breakwater. Turmoil. Water like broken glass.

Ms Della Gira continues gravely with her task. Her long black hair hangs in ropes around her face and arms, stirred by the rhythm of the spinning. Her eyes are still, cast down, her fine lashes brush against the twin grey hollows of her cheeks, and Brenda gasps. That twisting and turning magical hand has worked a transformation. Miraculous. All red streaks are gone and a huge light dome of palepink fluff has formed itself around the wooden wand. Brenda stretches out her hand as lightning cracks across the sea.

Quivering dome which glistens in the air. Ms Della Gira lifts up the magic wand, holding it out above the silver tub. 'Sir Lancelot,' she says, looking into Brenda's eyes while Brenda grabs the bit of stick still visible. A moment of ecstatic delight. She touches the hand of Ms Della Gira and stares back at her eyes. Then, with her free hand, Brenda moves coins across the counter, past dried starfish, racks of shells. Ms Della Gira adds them up, is satisfied, rings them into the till, deft and precise. She comes out from behind the counter, steps with grace across a pile of plastic crabs, a barrel of woven beach mats, three sombreros balanced on a promontory of calcite.

The two girls stand by the window. Brenda bites into the sticky vanishing candyfloss, sweet traces fading against her tongue and lips. Ms Della Gira pops into her mouth a bulbous notch of gum.

'Bad for business, this weather,' she mutters through chews. 'I don't believe that fucking rain.'

Brenda is enchanted by her silken voice.

Outside, on the deserted seafront, ornate railings are lashed by rain. The air's brim full of fallen petals, the flowerbeds in the promenade gardens stripped of colour. A vast zigzag of lightning seems to rip the window from side to side. Vinyl seaweed shimmers in a heap by the door. In the lit up moment Ms Della Gira holds tightly onto Brenda's arm, then the promenade shop goes dark.

'Hell', Ms Della Gira squawks. She's flurried and intense all in a burst, then sombre, quiet, remote, placing her right hand over her heart.

Brenda goes with the storm, spins through the repetitions of dark then light. Heavens seem to split and roar. She's intoxicated. Sight of the indigo sky, flash, flash. *As she rode down, as she rode down.* Sir Lancelot on her sleek white horse, its mane and tail like stippled silk. As they fly together across the strip of sand and then the sea, *she sings, tirra lirra.*

Adrift, spinning with the tide. Pools and eddies. All at sea. Brenda dreams of billowing robes, of chanting followed by silence, of Ms Della Gira in a tiny boat, her eyes shut tight. She's a dead but gleaming white. She swirls.

'I'm locking up now,' Ms Della Gira says suddenly, all brusque and matter of fact. She spits her gum into its paper, slings the moist little parcel behind the mound of plastic crabs, wipes her sticky hands on her T-shirt sleeves. 'Nobody'll come out in this.'

'No, I s'pose not,' admits Sir Brenda Lancelot, sad but realistic, as she turns her steed and canters over to the door.

'Goodbye.'

Waving with Rabbit

Here is the stage where Louise stands, feet slightly apart, one hand on hip, one hand in a gesture of introduction. Out there, where the audience sits, is darkness; Louise is in light. She moves in a circle of white light. In the audience there's laughter, in Louise an excluded and empty feeling, although she smiles. Just behind Louise the magician stands at a shiny lacquered table upon which is a tall conjuror's hat. It is this hat that Louise is pointing out to the audience. It is the hat from which many things emerge.

There always seems to be just another thing inside the hat after the last item has been pulled out,—the table is now littered with what has already been found. A bunch of flowers, a number of bright coloured scarves all knotted together, a horse-shoe, a mirror in a frame, a jug, a jar. The magician is holding the hat slanted towards the audience. It may seem empty but it's not. A clockwork frog leaps out, and springs a little way across the stage, causing more laughter. Then the orchestra strikes up and a small red curtain comes down and covers the table and the hat because they're no longer part of the action and must vanish quickly, smoothly, so as not to impede the flow of the act. A final brassy blare as a long box is brought on to centre stage.

Now the magician's taken over, he's the one introducing. He holds up one of Louise's hands towards the darkness out there and the audience contained inside it. There's a dramatic silence as he tells them he is to saw up Louise into pieces, then try to put her back together again. *Try.* The audience cheers. This is the big trick, the one they've been waiting for. Seen it before of course, it's one of the oldest tricks, but still carries allure. Louise in her heels and fishnets, her glimmering leotard, bows to the audience in her turn, and is led, as drums roll, to the long box on the floor. This is Louise's moment. Everybody's out there and staring right at her. *Is she real or isn't she?* Louise, bowing once more, steps into the box and the lid is closed. *Is Louise really inside the box? Does Louise exist?* The magician takes up a silver saw.

Dismemberment and restitution.

Louise and Jon, the magician, are staying in a chalet in the Holiday Park. They've come to Tenerife for the Season, to do their Magic Show. The magician is going blind, this booking is probably their last. They will be leaving the day after tomorrow, going back to Jon's flat on the outskirts of Maidstone. Louise sighs, picturing this.

At the back of the chalet is a paved in area where they keep the rabbit-hutch. It seems funny to Louise that there's a rabbit-hutch here in Tenerife. The rabbit-hutch seems to belong to Maidstone and the rabbit too. The rabbit is white with pink eyes, its name is Rabbit, there's a look to it which says *suburbs,* rows of small rectangular gardens with nettles in the corner, a cosiness, a slight ungainliness, a homely innocence. The rabbit belongs to the outskirts of somewhere, Louise feels a degree of empathy. She herself is never quite centre-stage, even when she's being sawn apart.

Louise has faced the hutch to the wall to give shade. Now, it's evening, Rabbit is having its run, or its awkward bobbity jog, across the concrete patch. Louise has spread a few leaves about to make it nicer. She strokes Rabbit's ears. Louise and Rabbit have another things in common, they're both here to work not just be decorative, they are shown to the audience as examples of ordinary living things at the end of the magician's trick.

The only difference is Louise has been put back together and Rabbit appears out of *thin air,* out of the magician's hat. All they have to do is convince the audience they are real and not just an appearance.

Louise is afraid of change. She knows it, but can't seem to overcome the fear. Even the word is daunting. *Change.* It makes her feel all loose and unconnected. Stroking Rabbit's ears she remembers she'd first felt that way when her father had disappeared. She'd come home from school and there was her mother with serious eyes, meeting her by the front door. Her mother had said, 'Your father's done a disappearing act. I don't want to talk about it.' They never had really talked about it. Just two years later, when Louise was eleven, her mother died in a domestic accident where no foul play was suspected. In other words her mother was drunk, had fallen badly and choked on her own vomit. Louise had gone to live with an older cousin whom she thought of as an aunt. That loose and unconnected feeling has been with Louise for a long time. She puts Rabbit on the ground and he bobs off across the concreted square in search of possible grass. She sees his white fast-leaping body in the darkness. She hopes that Rabbit feels something like happiness.

Walking out on the beach of white sand. Mid-day, the sky's so blue. Louise, sorry the time's come to be leaving here. She tries to think of Maidstone, of Jon's plain flat on the ground-floor of a house on a road to nowhere. Or nowhere that matters to Louise. What she thinks is, most people are not at the centre of a place but exist on the margins, clinging to the edge of something but not actually inside it. The feeling she's not alone doesn't comfort her, it just makes her feel more ordinary. Flat beach of hot white sand, her feet sting with the impact of each tread. Quite a few things bother Louise. Being out on the margins is one of them, knowing that a hoard of other people are there with her is another. The fast change of things, or maybe even more, the slow change you're not aware is happening. That is worse, it's like a deception. But walking along by the sea, she's happy. Her heels sink comfortingly into burning sand at each footfall, the hot grains fall away grittily as her feet press down.

It's a moment when she can push away troubled thoughts and just be. There aren't enough of those. Looking up she sees Jon walking on the path next to the beach, not so far away; she can see his frown. It draws the pleasure of the moment away from her. And he seems distracted as though he's not seeing anything around him. He's leaning forward and moving quickly, the way he always walks. It's the reason she never goes for walks with him. Louise calls out, a heavy pain striking inside her. He stops abruptly, as though pulled up. Looks her way, but not quite, the frown now a squint, sun's in his eyes. He puts up a hand. *Down here,* she calls and he waves in response. But he hasn't seen her. She sees him trying to focus on where her voice came from, straining to make out her image. *A blind man,* she says to herself. *This is how it will be.* Sometime soon he will never see her again. It makes her feel alone, it makes her feel less than alone. As though part of her has kept on existing because he has been her witness. He's caught sight of her at last, waves as if she's at least a mile off. Maybe that's the way it seems to him. She is fuzzy, blurred about the edges, blending in with the landscape, hardly here at all. She waves back, sees his eyes concentrating on her arm movement, thinking that though he's pleased to see her because it means he can see and because it means she can see him seeing so she won't pity him, he isn't pleased to see *her.* No, the frown's still there. Their love has got so mixed up with pride and pain, and habitualisation because they've been together over nine years now, it's almost invisible. Louise is smiling, though she wants to cry.

Here is the box where Louise will lie to be sawn in half. The audience are cheering, she understands their hope that it will and will not happen; the need for a trick, the need for reality. The reality here would be a severed torso and blood. Louise knows the ambivalence of the audience. She walks to the box. The magician has lifted the lid and tilted the box towards the audience so they can see for themselves it really is quite ordinary, there's nothing hidden inside. Just a flowered silky lining. A coffin or a music-case. Now Louise is stepping inside, the band playing, accompanying her. She's inside, her head protruding from a hole at the top end. At the other end fish-netted legs stick out, high-heels on the feet. The magician walks round the box fastening locks, talking to the audience. Louise knows their speculations will have started. *No, there must be two people, Louise at the top of the box and somebody else squeezed into the bottom part. Louise isn't there at all, it's a dummy. No two midgets, that's how they can both get in that box. The box isn't big enough for two normal size Louises. But the legs don't look like midget's legs. The legs are fake.* But when the Magician takes up the saw, to the roll of drums, there's still a whispered hush. Because, *there's a chance the saw could slip. Things could go very wrong, you never know.* There could be a massacre.

Louise has a picture of Maidstone life. She'll go shopping alone as she always does but it will be raining. She is affected by the weather, it's difficult for her to function in the semi-dark. She thinks of grey afternoons, she thinks of skirting puddles, of being mud splattered by cars passing fast along the highway. Thinks of arriving at the dismal flat where there will be a blind man waiting, a stranger, thinks of running away. She's been with Jon for nearly ten years. They've travelled about mostly, done seasonal work in sunny places, magic shows on cruises for the old and young. In between they've usually stayed in her flat in Nottingham, a flat she has recently given up. His home on the outskirts of Maidstone was rented out, now it will be *their* home. But where to run? And then she feels guilty for even thinking the word *run.* Run. Away from a blind man, the one she loves? And why does she think of Jon as a stranger? If only she could banish the words from her mind, make the thoughts behind the words just disappear, and then resurrect them as the sweet fresh feelings she used to have.

Illusion. The trick has happened. Louise is cut and restored. She is standing up and showing her whole body to the audience. Mauve satin thighs, black laced. She does her drawling body sway from left to right, from right to left. Bows the audience into the final trick. The magician is taking up his hat from the table preparatory to saying goodbye. *Goodbye* is on his lips, it's in his movements. But wait, there's something more to be found. He lifts the hat, holding the interior out towards the auditorium. Puts in his hand and fishes out Rabbit where there was no rabbit before. Audience clapping and laughing. A nice touch, nice finish. Nice touching finish. Rabbit is held high and then passed to Louise, the magician takes centre stage. He bows. Louise just next to him bows also. Just next to but a thousand miles away. Here on the sidelines as the curtain goes down, as the curtain goes up. As the band twangs their moment and phases them out, as the clapping rises up and ceases. Louise, waving with Rabbit as the curtain goes down. Down.

Louise, wanting Jon to think, no not to think, to just love her as she wants to be loved. For it all to be happening—the magical turmoil of love. She needs to be persuaded it's real. One of the pictures always present in her mind is of legs kicking, legs that are not hers. Kicking and kicking high to prove they are alive. Not that they're her legs, she doesn't think they are. But then everything is a confusion in this life. At the end of the day any thing at all is possible, anything can be negated. Louise is not Louise, the box is not a box.

Final bow and curtain and Louise is thinking, Perhaps I'm to blame for the feeling of uncertainty about everything, maybe it's just because I can't believe that feelings really do exist. Out of the two of us, it's you who are the believer. As you stretch arms up and out, as you command the audience with your eyes. What a con that is, my love. You can hardly see. Though you've half convinced yourself you have the power to bring your sight back.

I'll admit I'm torn, what I really need is for you to convince me that love at least is real. I don't want it to be pity that keeps me here now, keeps me ducking and diving, keeps me hidden away and then revealed, and when revealed, keeping on with the empty smiling. Living a life of appearances. Oh I could manage it, you could say it's not so much to give. But it's so silent in the Maidstone night. Everyone will have gone away; it'll be just you and your bitter looks and me. You are more bitter than you were a year ago. It can't be easy to accept the idea of being blind. How will things be then? You *say* you love me but isn't that just a word?

In the still afternoon Louise calls Jon across to save her from these worst of thoughts, to create a little warmth for both of them. He falls onto and into her, they slide together between the sheets.

Today is the day of the last show. The last show ever, or the last show here? *Forever,* of course, Louise says to herself, as Jon pulls himself up and away from her, the act over quickly as though it's a thing of no importance, as though there are few new discoveries to make. Forever is a hard word to hear even when it's only she herself who's said it. It means there's a change about to happen that there will be no coming back from.

She and Jon don't talk about his coming blindness and Louise knows she's partly responsible for their avoidance, that she really can't bear hearing Jon's hurt and painful thoughts. She wants the thoughts to go away, wants him to not have them, wants him only to be happy. Otherwise it's an agony to her. Her heart beats wild with chaos, she loses her life rhythm, sees her life in pieces. The words *her life* are like bits of broken glass she tries her best to hang on to. But she's bleeding every time she thinks them. She looks at Jon, hoping he feels at peace, at least that. Right now he's getting up out of bed, humming a light tune. The tune consoles her; her second of frenzy fades down. Jon's gone into the small kitchen to make coffee, Louise can see him through two doorways. It's as if he's on a stage and Louise is in the auditorium watching his performance. He takes the kettle over to the tap, the water misses, sprays him, she hears him laugh and swear. A nice and nasty moment keeping Louise's subterranean agony at bay but not letting her escape its shadow.

Now here is Louise bringing dandelion leaves for Rabbit. She shuts the chalet door behind her, walks over to the hutch, but the hutch is empty. Louise starts getting a loose and unsettled feeling. *Rabbit,* she calls in a quaking voice. *Where are you?* But there's nothing, no sign or movement. The hutch is quite empty, she examines the open wire fronted part where Rabbit comes out when he wants to be sociable and the hidden away part, by opening up the top. She stares at each corner. Nothing. Tears spring into her eyes. She can't begin to think what's happened. *Rabbit?* That's the only word Louise can say. At first, only silence, then there's a shuffling and a scuffling and she sees his familiar little white puffed out shape hopping along by the fence. She'd forgotten to put Rabbit away, he's been out here for hours. There are wild creatures about, the fence wouldn't keep them out. She knows that and feels bad. But anyway it's all okay. Louise holds out a leaf and Rabbit bobs over and tugs at it chewing with a jerky motion, his pink rimmed eyes serene. No sad endings then, for this Louise feels grateful. And yes, Rabbit lives on to be pulled out of the magician's hat, ears first, one more time.

This is the night when someone will take a photo that Louise will keep. Louise will never cease to feel comfort when she looks at it. She'll show it to everyone who comes round to the Maidstone flat. And anyway, she doesn't have to show. It's there for all to see, standing above the fireplace in a polished frame. In the photo Louise is standing with Rabbit in the crook of her arm. She's smiling broadly and Rabbit would be too if he could, the picture shows that clearly. Rabbit is happy. Louise and Rabbit will go through all eternity like this. Nothing that really matters can ever change.

Monkey Face

A coin in my hand, held up between my fingers like a crisp silver moon. Now it's gone again, too fast for you to see. The most real part of me lives in the palm of my hand, a hidden self that I conjure up out of nothing. I like to surprise you, suddenly becoming visible. For this I have to get the timing right, be spot on.

Look, there's a coin behind your ear. I draw it out while you blink, puff it off and away to nothing. You smile at me with your scrunched up *monkey* face your one year old eyes happy to accept magic as a natural thing.

An afternoon which has this taste of September to it. In the air, in the food. The garden colours are mauve and whitish grey. Late summer wasps, grass going to the seedy stage, sneeze dust, a dryness to everything. The world is treading down to straw. Andrew and I talking at the table, laughter taking account of endings, becoming precious to us. It's nothing like the sound of clear cut happiness. You in your baby chair tasting apple, a puckered look. *Nice*, we say and make a *mmm mmm* noise.

There will be endings because there have to be. What's started now can't be circumvented. It would be easy to say the words, *We're alright now. Let's begin again. We're alright.* Too easy to be true.

Because after the words had been said, even if they were said and meant, what's started would still be going on, say what you like about making a firm decision. Would still be going on, though no decision had been made. As if what's been started knows it's the future, the way ahead, even if we ourselves aren't so certain. Mind you, we are certain when we laugh across the table. We know then this moment is to be short lived. I can't allow myself to feel guilty about what I'm doing. Or, perhaps I can, but it makes no difference either and so I push it off. Why go through the guilt when I know I'm still going ahead with leaving? Andrew is especially good with you, chopping up your food, catching blobs of it that come back out of your mouth again on the side of your bib. As though he's saying to me, *Look what you'll be breaking up here, a good father-daughter relationship.* I am sober watching him, because it's true. He pats at your hair, as though he's saying to you, *Remember me here today doing this.* Of course he could have kept in touch, but he went off to New Zealand and we hardly heard from him. You saw him the once. He came over when his mother died. A sparse man in a puffy coat. You were ten, he was a stranger. I'm not saying it isn't sad.

I'd met Gilby you see, remember Gilby? Your dad and I had had our troubles, we were shaky from the beginning, and then Gilby, our relationship couldn't survive that. And Gilby. He kind of fleshed out all the fantasies of my life as I did his. Strange it didn't last, very likely we burned each other out. There was no going back of course. I can only say I'm sorry.

So for the next few years it was just you and me. We tried to make light of the intensity of that, acting casual in front of your friends, me being more typically *motherlike* in front of mine. But we were in secret complicity, locked tight like twins in special understanding. You were bound to be resentful when I met Mark. Jealousy made you hate him, yet there was relief too. I saw it in your eyes when you realised Mark was serious. A lightening, as though some great weight had been lifted. The love between us was always desperate adoration and desperate burden in equal mix.

From around the time you were two and a half there were no men in my life, our involvement was undiluted. You were my companion on outings to the city centre. We loved those, both of us. So many café tables we've sat at, me with my cappuccino, you with orange juice with bits. Slices of pizza, with extra pepperoni, no mushrooms. You were always so particular about what you liked and didn't like. When everything was perfect you'd make your monkey face, half smile, half frown, - the frown part of it I always thought meant you'd already seen that nothing lasts forever.

After Andrew and after Gilby we went on holiday. Soon you'd be three. Suitcases to trundle, the baby buggy, it was hard to cope but I was happy though I'd expected to be sad. We went to The Isle of Wight and in this café I said to you to sit with all the stuff, and to the waitresses to watch you, I'd be two minutes hailing a taxi from the rank I'd just seen a bit further on. I was one minute, the taxi lurching in my wake, and you weren't there. I ran out into the street with a dry hollow heart afraid to think, gouging my nails into the palms of my hands, my jaw extending forward stiffly. I let out these grunting noises, regularly spaced, trying to force out thoughts this way, keep myself clear of them. Because I didn't want to be normal, to do things in the normal way, I didn't want to register the horror reaching out at me. My life was on hold those nightmarish few moments as I raced up and down the street. Smell of salt and fish wrappers, crunch of gravelly sand, every innocent thing seeming to hold despair inside itself though I tried not to see it like that. *Monkey Face, Oh Monkey Face.* Then there you were, surrounded by this group of happy frail ladies. Happy with you they were, in your banana and lemon holiday dress, your round cherubic arms, your bright eyes and question mark of a smile and baby chatter. I had to humour them in taking you away, you were too much to part with even for strangers.

You reach out and touch my hand, a knowing look to you, as if you're seeing things I just don't notice and you can't or won't tell me. A secret. You like to keep something up your sleeve. Later in our hotel room you slip behind the curtains. *Now you see me now you don't.* You peep out at me with your liquid eyes. One, two, you blink. I am soft with longing, a rabbit you pull out of your hat to cuddle. You stroke my hair, mollify my ears. You are always fresh with your tricks, I can never quite keep up with you. The more I look the less I see.

The Gold-Road

The swimmers walk with rolled towels. Cross the bare
flowerbeds on the promenade gardens, climb the railings, jump
down onto the beach. They land together, falling forward and
laughing, brushing the moist clogs of sand from their anoraks.
A cold fine day with this icy white quality to it, a sky of pale
china blue. Here they are on the sand which is dense, cold,
uninviting. Sharp air catches at their laughter, they go to the
water's edge.

The towels are spread and the two swimmers are sitting and
looking up at the winter sky. Behind them the seafront with
its row of arcades, the straight wide road and incessant cars.
To the front of them the sea, eel silver, choppy grey. That swish-
ing slap and roar of waves. And here they sit, in a little haven
of blue and yellow beach towels, replicating summer. Emma and
Lou, friends since school, always sharing this need to be different, to go against the grain. Winter swimmers, shivering in
the wind. Now, as they sit by the sea Emma is wondering why
she is doing this, but Lou, motivated by the challenge, feels an
easy determination. Time to swim. They pull off their outer
clothes.

What am I trying to prove? thinks Emma. Lou is looking back at the promenade road with dislike and hardly thinking at all.

They stand together in the shallows adjusting to the feel of the sea. It gushes over their feet, and their ears are bursting with noise, with the boom and crash of the waves. Their skin is purplish now, vivid with the cold, and saltiness is already everywhere, their eyes smart with it. But Emma, to her surprise, has begun to feel a tremor of excitement. *Yes,* she's thinking. *After all, it is worth it, worth the agony.* And Lou stands staunch and purposeful keeping her body tight against the wind, never before so conscious of how precious this friendship is to her.

Emma and Lou have thought of themselves as *the swimmers* ever since they started coming out all the year round. Today they left home in the usual way, walked down the street, crossed the promenade and came within sight of the sea. Nothing was different, they just did what they always did. It was as two swimmers that they climbed the railings and jumped down to the beach. But strangely, perhaps mystically, this is a turning point. Sometimes, without warning, the world *does* change in this way.

'I'm not going in,' Lou suddenly announces. 'It's too cold,' she says lamely, sounding puzzled herself. Her voice has a rapid quality to it as though she's hunting for a reason. She stands stiffly, feeling tragic and miserable, sensing endings and coming loss, but also a pure cold resistance. She's almost in tears. *Why should she swim? Just because she always does? Emma shouldn't expect, just because they have always been friends, just because . . .* her thought cannot finish itself, she knows it is not reasonable.

'Why are you saying this now, at the last minute?' Emma's voice is loud, very clear and precise. It seems as if the rush of sea has ceased for a moment to let her speak, as though the beach, the tide, maybe the whole of the universe itself, is waiting with her for Lou's reply. It does not come. The pressure is too great and Lou looks straight at Emma, not averting her eyes, but speechless. A long moment of silence between them as though destiny has not yet been decided, then Emma turns and walks

waist deep into the sea. She's feeling abandoned, almost lost.
'It's not bad,' she calls through chattering teeth, and she looks
back at Lou. Lou standing with the water lapping round her
ankles, her eyes gone dark as anything. Strip of beige sand
behind her, gunmetal railings, bare gardens, the road where a
line of cars is passing up and down. Frame of buildings, a hill,
the sky. To the right a bleak promontory with three bare trees,
to the left the shadowy curve of the breakwater. Emma looks
unhurriedly at all these things and then back at Lou's defiant-
dark eyes. *Why do you have to be so dramatic?* she thinks, criti-
cally. Then she turns her face to the sea, throws her body
forward into the cold water and starts to swim. Pushing her
arms into agony, into dark liquid ice. Entering into it and
through it.

Heading out. She sees Lou through the gap between her
raised left arm and the sea, Lou walking away along the sand
her hair gleaming like a brass halo in a flash of winter sun.
Emma feels starkly alone, the retreating round brass head looks
impervious. *I'll get out of the water. We'll walk together to that breakwater*, she's thinking desperately, but almost at the same
moment she notices that the sea is warm and that her body is
cutting keenly through its silky texture. The sun shines out
brightly now just ahead of her, makes a golden path across the
sea, and she knows with this deep certainty that she will travel
along it.

The breath flows down into her, then up and out. Flowing
into, and up and out. Left arm, right arm, inward flowing
breath. Up and out. Water like silk, the frill of foam. Saltiness.
Left arm, right arm. Flow-ow-ow, of breath. Up, out. Out. Silk,
white, salt. Left, right. Flow. And there's this long golden path
which links her to the horizon. From her own tiny section of the
sea she feels connected to the sky, and to everything. Left, right,
flow, gold. As one.

Lou has walked to the breakwater and stands now at the bottom
of a little flight of steps cut into the stone. She feels this huge
excitement as if the steps will lead her somewhere mysterious.
And these steps will be an escape route from oh so many terrible

things, like habits which imprison the spirit, and from pain and loss and knowledge of defeat. She has this strange crazy feeling that nature has defeated her but civilisation will save her. This idea makes her happy, it makes her laugh. To have been wrong about so many things and to have found it out and to not mind. Now she's climbing, feeling dynamic, feeling light footed, sure of herself, seeing with pleasure that the centre of each stone step is worn down by the rubbing of many feet.

She feels the past through contact with the stone and gets this sense of harmony. How wonderful to be treading these steps and to be a part of history. And the solid contact with the stone. That is the now, and the future is an enchanting mystery. *Perhaps I'm not a swimmer,* she thinks as she goes, and she gets this surge of happiness at being able to question the validity of things. All the time she's climbing up through the brightness and the wind to the summit of the breakwater, and each step that she takes has the lightness to it of a right, rare freedom newly found. Higher and higher she goes, her face held full to the wind.

Acknowledgements

The author would like to thank the editors of the following publications where some of the stories from this collection first appeared:

Monkey Face in *Cadenza*, 2007
Chicken eye in *Snow Monkey*, 2006
Lady of the Spin in *Stand*, 2006
Chicken eye in *The New Writer*, 2005
Blue Movie in *Staple*, 2005
The Other Side of Diane in *Mslexia*, 2005
Salamander in *Night Train*, 2005
Yellow Plastic Shoe in *The London Magazine*, 2005
Tailbacks in Spiked, 2004
The Sadness Story in *Staple*, 2003
Tango in *Nomad*, 2002
The Gold Road in *The Interpreter's House*, 2002
Billie-Ricky in *Staple*, 2001
The Outsider in *Multi-Storey*, 2001

Printed in the United Kingdom
by Lightning Source UK Ltd.
120635UK00001B/229-255